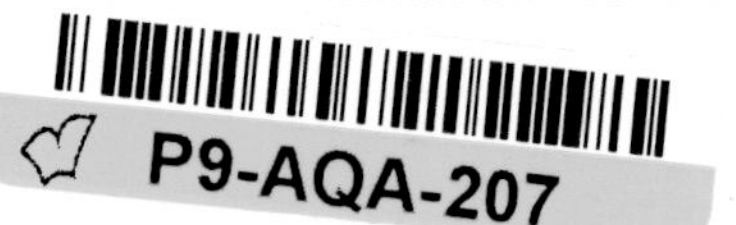

TAKE A CHANCE ON ME

"A BBW Romance"

BY CHELLY P

This is a work of fiction. All of the characters, organizations, and events portrayed in this novel are either products of the author's imagination or are used fictitiously. Any resemblance to actual persons, living or dead is purely coincidental.

TPD
The Plugs Daughter

JOIN MAILING LIST!!
For Upcoming Releases, Sneak Peeks Contest and More...
bit.ly/3kwDoXB

Synopsis

Life always throws you curveballs, something both Lovely and Craft can tell you from first hand experience.

Craft, A deprived boy who has witnessed life's cruel take on love, now a man ready to experience the peace that devotion should bring.
Lovely, a girl constantly put down by her peers, who's blossomed into a woman. Not ashamed of her beautiful hershey kissed skin, and plus size frame, Lovely is ready to take over the world. When Craft lays eyes on the plus size beauty, and is ready to stake his claim one obstacle seems to deter him. However, when his mind is made up he's all for the challenge.

With an aura of an angel, and heart of gold any man would be lucky to have her by his side. The question is, will the feelings be reciprocated? Ride with Lovely and Craft in this beautifully told story and watch first hand how two strangers heart collide and romance unfolds.

Chapter 1

Lovely

"Welcome to Stylez by Lovely where you can get your hair styled, nails fly, brows plucked, and the whole nine. How can we help you today?" My little sister, Gorgeous, greeted a customer as they entered the salon.

"Yeah, where is Lovely?" The customer questioned.

"Do you have an appointment with her, or are you trying to book an appointment?"

"Little girl, do you see my hair? Does it look like I need Lovely doing anything for me?" A lady questioned loudly.

"Well, since you asked, yes, it looks like you need the works done by Lovely!" Gorgeous smartly responded.

"Little bitch, don't get cute!"

"I'm sorry, please give me a moment to check on the front." I apologized to my client as I placed her under the dryer.

I quickly made my way out of the washroom because my salon was not the place for negativity, but no one would disrespect my little sister.

"Listen, I don't know who you are, or what your business is here today, but you gone watch how you talk to this one!" My stylist/best friend since we were thirteen, Wise, was in a lady's face.

My salon was a peaceful oasis. Many women came here

to get pampered and relax. I took pride in my salon because it was not just a hair shop. We had six hair stylists, three nail technicians, two wax specialist, two masseuses, two loc specialists, and three make-up artists. Wise was one of the stylists to do all six. I was a hairstylist and MUA, and two of my other hair stylists were versatile in two other skills. The beautiful thing about my shop was that several men frequented the salon.

"Girl, if you don't take your baby and get the hell out of here!" Wise was in her face, waving a curling iron that I was sure she was using on her client.

"Hello, I'm Lovely. How can I help you today?" I questioned as I approached the receptionist booth. It was made up of a glass display case that housed hair products and a rolling chair that Gorgeous just had to have.

She took a moment to look me up and down. "Where is Glen?"

"I'm sorry, but we don't have a Glen that works here. The barbershop is at the end of the block. You can maybe try there." I smiled at her and prepared to head back to my client, but in my mind, I was just hoping she was not talking about my Glen.

"You and I both know Glen doesn't do hair. In fact, he is a police officer," she snapped.

"I'm sorry, but again, there is no Glen that works here. If Glen is a police officer, then you should be at the police station looking for him. Now if you are not here trying to make an appointment, you have a good day. I hope you find Glen." Relief kind of filled me because my Glen worked in banking.

"No, I came to the right place, looking for our Glen. You see, Glen knows I'm going out of town today. The two of you are supposed to keep our son, Glen Aiden James Jr." She spoke, snatching the cover off the baby.

It suddenly got hot, and for a moment, I felt like I was going to vomit. That baby had Glen's whole face.

"This bitch has lost her damn mind!" Wise mumbled from the side of me.

"Yeah, bitch, I can see it all in your face. You know for a fact now that I'm talking about your Glen. Well, really, he's our Glen. But I haven't been able to get in touch with Glen for two days, and I need to finish getting ready for my trip. So, I thought who better than his stepmother to leave my son with?" She spoke with a smirk on her face, but her and Glen both had me fucked up.

"My best friend is not the type to fight, but, bitch, I'm about to whoop your ass!" Wise snatched her up before I could stop her.

This moment was all too much. Wise was beating this girl, and I didn't feel bad about it. But then, this baby was screaming at the top of its lungs. The salon was full of clients. This was not what I was about.

"Get her off me!" The girl cried out.

"Kevin!" I called out to the only male hairstylist we had. "Please help me get Wise." I instructed as I attempted to get her off this girl.

"She needs a good ass whooping, coming in here with this mess," Kevin spoke, pulling Wise off the girl.

"You're going to jail. Do you know who my man is?" The girl ranted while getting off the floor.

"Glen isn't a police officer, dummy. You're laying up with a man that you know nothing about. Wait, my bad, you know he has a woman." Wise huffed.

"Look, you need to get your baby and leave." I pointed between her and the door. "This is my place of business, and we don't carry on like this here."

"Like I said, since I can't get a hold of Glen, the baby will be staying with your big ass!"

"Sweetheart, if you leave that baby here, I will be calling the police and notifying them that you abandoned your baby. Now again, you need to leave."

"You and I both know your big, passive ass won't call the damn police. You should be happy I gave Glen something he really wanted. I mean, since we both know you can't give him kids."

"Okay, that's enough. Boss lady asked you to leave, so you need to go."

I stood, frozen, as Kevin ushered her out, along with her baby.

"Hey, go take a moment. I'll get someone to finish your client." Wise hugged me.

I hugged her back and took a deep breath. "No, it's okay. I got it."

"You sure?" She pulled back, looking me in my eyes.

It was the end of July, and our back-to-school special had begun, causing the shop to be overly busy and crowded. Not only were some of our regulars present, but we also had a few new and returning kids, along with their parents.

"Yes." I pulled away and went to finish with my client.

Everyone got back to work, and no one mentioned the incident, but you could tell it was on everyone's mind. I provided lunch for the whole salon and provided fifteen percent off to all clients that were getting their hair done during the commotion. After the last client had been serviced, and all stylists and techs were gone, it was Wise and me doing the final cleaning and prepping for Monday. Gorgeous had left long ago to spend the remainder of her weekend at her best friend's house.

"Now that everything is to your liking, let's go get a bite to eat and a few drinks." Wise spoke, plopping down in her chair and swirling around.

"I really don't want to, but we both know you won't take no for an answer." I took a seat in the chair next to hers.

"It's nine on a Saturday night. We're going to the strip club. Wings, drinks, and us shaking a little something." Wise danced in her chair.

"I'm beginning to think you have something to tell me."

"Yeah, that ain't no wings like a strip club wings, baby!" She laughed.

I tried my hardest not to laugh, but I just couldn't hold it in. So, I laughed right along with her.

While I was the thinker, always second guessing myself and hesitating to try new things, Wise was carefree, a risk taker, liable to pop off at any moment, and always the life of the party. Many people had questioned our friendship over the years, but without her, I wouldn't have this salon today. In fact, I probably wouldn't be here today. She had been my saving grace many days. Growing up, I was always bigger than the other kids. Well, fatter in their words. There wasn't a day that I didn't come home crying to my mother about what the kids said about me and what they may have done to me. My mother would just rock me in her arms and tell me how beautiful I was while my grandmother would tell me to whoop one of their asses one good time and everyone would leave me alone. Then, my grandmother would go up to the school each time and raise hell.

I remember when I was thirteen, my mother passed away during the birth of my little sister, Gorgeous, leaving myself and Gorgeous in the care of my grandmother. Up until that point, my father was the type to drop by when he felt like it, but he made sure I was taken care of financially. But after my mother's passing and the birth of my sister, his presence in my life changed. I remembered him showing up to the hospital, and the man that he was always seemed to be frowning and serious about something. But not this time. He stood over my mother's body silently for a while, then he came to sit beside me. I looked up at him, and I saw the tears rolling down his face. He tried to take care of my sister and I on his own for about two months, but after constantly calling my grandmother over for every little thing, they felt it was best we lived with my grandmother full time. As for Gorgeous' father, he never made it to the hospital on the day of her birth nor to my mother's funeral. In fact, he was non-existent except for the checks that were sent, but they eventually stopped. He was in the service and felt from the start that she would be better off with my grandmother. Between my father, grandmother, and my Papa Nelson, my father's father, and the many aunts that I had on my dad's side, me and Gorgeous were well loved and taken care of.

Moving in with my grandmother meant a new junior high and a new set of kids to be bullied by in the middle of my eighth-grade year. Now, I may have been bigger than the other kids, but my momma kept me dressed. We would have these mother daughter days every other Saturday. We would go to the nail shop, hair shop, and then end the day with dinner at a restaurant. Even with my mother passing, my grandmother made sure to get me to the salon and nail shop every other Saturday. At my old school, I was picked on for being fat and my skin being too dark. I inherited my mother's beautiful, dark skin color, slightly bubbled eyes, and nose that started slender but widened at the bottom, but I got my full lips and bushy eyebrows from my father. My size came from both sides of the family. My father was a big guy - tall and wide. My mother was a beautiful, full-figured woman, so me being bigger than the other kids was inevitable.

At my new school, the kids picked at me for being black, dark as coal as they called it, and fat, and they felt I thought I was better than them and a nerd. My cousin, Abiri, who my grandmother raised since he was two after his mother and father were gunned down, was getting in trouble every week for defending me. My grandmother only encouraged him to continue. It wasn't until a girl thought it would be funny to cut my hair, and I finally did what my grandmother had been telling me to do. I beat her up, but her sister and cousin decided to jump in. That was the day me and Wise became friends. She jumped in as well as my cousin. So, as we sat in the office, me missing half a ponytail, waiting for my grandmother and Wise's mother, we officially introduced ourselves and had been stuck together ever since. The kids still said stuff here and there, but no one ever touched me again.

"That's right, friend. Let these skinny hoes know that us big girls ain't shit to play with. Shake that shit, friend." Wise stood behind me, yelling loudly and smacking my butt as I bounced it to the beat of the song. I made the dip in my back deeper and bounced everything my momma blessed me with.

An hour and a half in, a tray of wings, and I didn't know how many drinks, I was feeling good, like a different person.

"Here, drink this." Wise shoved a drink in my hand as the song ended.

"Oh, my God, what is this?" I took two sips and knew I wasn't going to finish it.

"Tokyo tea!" She started dancing as the beat of the next song started to play.

"Nope, that's too strong." I shook my head, sitting the drink on the table.

"Nope, you said we would have a good night. Drink this and finish showing these looking ass hoes and drooling niggas that ain't shit sweet about you. Wait, never mind. I'm talking about you and not me." She laughed before downing her drink.

I rolled my eyes at her before drinking mine as well.

"Okay, that's enough. I can't drink anything else. But I do need to go to the bathroom."

"Yes, I need to go too."

After our bathroom run, on the way back to our table, I took the opportunity to take in everything. My eyes veered over to the stage, and momentarily, I got caught up watching the current performer and wasn't paying attention to where I was going. I walked right into someone.

"Excuse me, my apologies. I got caught up in watching the dancer." I looked up at the man I bumped into, offering my apologies.

Grunting, he looked from me to the stage and back at me. "Fat ass probably wishes that could be you up there, huh?"

"Excuse me?" I wasn't even offended or shocked. I was plus sized and loved every part of me - my 42GG breasts, stomach that protruded, thighs that molded to my 4x pants, and a butt that was going to wave at you when I walked by.

"Bitch boy, watch how you talk to this one. Be glad she even apologized to your sorry ass," Wise spat from behind me.

"Aww, shit, not tonight, dog. She apologized. Don't make it

bigger than what it is." A guy spoke from behind him.

"Nah, if she wasn't so fat, maybe she wouldn't have bumped into me in the first place."

"If I were you, I would take my homeboy's advice and shut up." Wise attempted to step in front of me.

"Wise, let's just go. I apologized, and that's all I have to offer him." I attempted to move past him.

"Well, I got some advice for your big ass." He grabbed my arm.

"You must have lost your mind grabbing on her!" Wise shouted.

"The lady bumped into you, and she also apologized to you. Take your hands off her and let her go on her way." I looked up at the beautiful gentlemen as he spoke.

"Craft?" The guy quickly released my arm and backed away.

"Any man that can be tough with a woman but cowers in front of another man is a bitch. But watch your step. Never know when you might step into your death." Wise hissed.

"Wise, Wise, don't make me call my boy because you are about to act up." The man turned his sights on Wise.

"You know these hands don't discriminate." Wise giggled.

"You ladies enjoy the rest of your night." He looked between the two of us.

"Thanks, Craft. Come on, Lovely." Wise grabbed my hand.

"Thank you so much." I spoke to the gentleman that helped me.

"No thanks needed, beautiful." He smiled at me before turning and walking away.

I stood there, watching him, until he joined his group of friends. He looked back in my direction, catching me staring. He smiled and winked at me. Embarrassed, I quickly turned and headed back to where we were seated with Wise giggling behind me.

"What?" I looked over my shoulder.

"Nothing, just observing you checking out a youngin'."

"What?"

"You don't even know who that is, do you?"

"No."

"One of the reasons we got banned from going to Papa's gym."

I looked back in my handsome savior's direction, and he was looking back at me. Quickly, I turned back to Wise.

"He doesn't look familiar."

"Yes, Lovely darling. He aged, just as you did. He was a little shorter, bonier, and definitely didn't have that facial hair."

I looked in his direction once again, and he was focused on whatever the guy sitting across from him was talking about. Just from his side profile, I could tell the gym worked in his favor.

"Stop staring and wipe the side of your mouth. You're drooling."

"No, I'm not." I wiped the side of my mouth, focusing back on Wise.

"Well, it looked like it from this angle." She laughed before intertwining our arms. "But one day, we were at the gym, not too long after we graduated high school. There was this young boy trying his hardest to get your number. Papa Nelson popped up out of nowhere and dragged him away by the back of his neck. All these years later, Abiri and I joke with him about it." I sat there for a moment, trying to remember, but I just couldn't. "You know Abiri's friend, Honor?"

"Yes, it's been a while since I've seen him though."

"That's actually his little cousin." Wise nodded in his direction.

"Oh." I looked over at him. "I see he's sitting with Jack cousin."

"Girl, fuck Jack. Jack is old news. I've moved onto bigger and better things, and trust, it's way better where I'm at now. I told you how after I caught Jack cheating, I pulled a him on him. Bitch ass couldn't take it, standing in the rain thinking he was Ray J. Went from asking why to calling me all types of bitches and hoes. Abiri had to put him on his ass when he thought he was going to buck at me."

"You told me about him cheating and you cheating back. But not all that other stuff."

"I didn't?"

"No, you didn't!"

"My bad."

"You haven't been telling me a lot of things lately." I scrunched my brows and rolled my eyes.

"What do you mean?"

"You didn't tell me there was someone new in your life. Although I picked up on it. The disappearing acts, lunch and flowers being delivered, smiling all in your phone."

"Don't nobody be disappearing." She waved me off.

"Well, you definitely haven't been sharing your whereabouts. But hey, enjoy your new boo. If you're happy, I'm happy, and you have been seeming more on the happy side lately." I wrapped my arm around her shoulder and hugged her.

"It's still new, but I am happy."

"That's all that matters, and when you're ready, I'll be ready to meet him and make sure he's right for you and to let him know not to play with you."

"Oh, I think he knows." She smiled and winked. "We may as well close out our tab and call it a night."

"I'm staying with you tonight." I yawned.

"You need to go home and put Glen conniving behind out."

"I just want to get some good sleep tonight. Well, this morning."

She flagged the waitress over to close out our tab. As we made our way out of the strip club, I turned once more to get one last look at the gentleman, only to find that his eyes were on me. Smiling at him, he smiled back with a slight nod.

Ring, ring. Ring, ring.

I heard my phone going off, but this sleep was just too amazing. Not to mention, the gentleman from last night made an appearance. After my phone stopped ringing and started back up, I finally felt around for it with my eyes still closed. It stopped ringing and started up once again before I finally had it in my hands.

"Hello."

"Lovely, where are you?" Glen yelled into the phone frantically. "I waited up until three this morning, waiting on you, and I've been calling your phone. I went to sleep and woke up, and you still didn't make it home."

"Glen, can you please stop yelling?" I sighed.

"Stop yelling? It is eleven in the morning, and you're not home. Do you know how worried I am?"

"Not too worried." I mumbled.

"What?"

"Glen, I had a long night. I'll be home soon."

"You had a long night? Where are you?"

"Glen, I will see you when I get home." I hung up the phone before he could respond and rolled over, falling back to sleep.

Wise woke me up around two with lunch. I lounged around with her for a couple of hours, dreading going home. At around six, she dropped me off at my car, which I left parked at the salon. Before we parted ways, she made me promise I would call her if things went south with Glen.

On my way home, I called my sister to check in with her. She let me know that she would be staying the night at her best friend's house again, and they would be going school shopping tomorrow. She had one week before her senior year began. Two weeks after my twenty-first birthday, my grandmother passed, leaving me to care for Gorgeous. I mean, I had my father, his side of the family, my cousin, Abiri, Wise, and her mother. Although my dad had his hiccups, there was a slight adjustment in him. He was a bit softer, and he didn't frown as much. It could have been the fact that he continually talked about time slipping away and losing out on something great. My grandfather would always say his stubbornness was haunting him. But when my grandmother passed, my father did step up in a major way, especially when it came to caring for Gorgeous.

My father always argued that he kept his distance at times due to the life he led. My father was a major player in guns distribution and drugs. So, he often stated he kept us at a distance to protect us. But he walked away from it all and went legit when we needed him the most. My grandmother's passing took a big toll on me. She battled with breast cancer silently. Her pastor presented Abiri and me each with letters that she left with him. She told us that she kept her sickness from us because she didn't want to be pumped full of medicine. She knew that we would do everything we could to keep her here. She said as much as she loved us, it was time to be back with her daughters. Although she wasn't here, she would always be looking over us. She left her house to both Abiri and I, but he signed the deed over to me solely. He had his life he was living and wanted to make sure Gorgeous and I were straight. She left me the building that once served as a market and pharmacy. I never had any idea that she purchased it. I converted that big, empty, open space into my now two-story, full-service oasis.

When you stepped inside the main level, there was the receptionist area and a few display cases with hair products, eight stations, six of which were occupied, and a beautiful shampoo room with four wash bowls and four dryers. Across from the shampoo room were the stairs that led to the second floor. Next to the shampoo room was my office, across from my office were two restrooms, men's and women's. Next to my office was the supply closet, which also housed a washer and dryer for these towels and aprons. On the second level, I had a big suite that housed four nail stations and two sinks, a suite with three make-up stations, two massage rooms, two rooms for waxing services, two bathrooms, an employee lounge, and another supply room. Abiri received our grandmother's flower shop. He purchased the building next to it and turned it into an auto/restoration shop.

Once arriving home, I sat in the car for ten minutes, talking to my sister. After hanging up with her, I sat in the car for ten more minutes, mentally preparing myself. Finally working up the courage, I got out of my car and made my way to the house. Before my foot could clear the first step, the front door swung open.

"I talked to you hours ago, and you're just now making it home?" Glen stood in the doorway, face red in anger.

"Let's go inside and talk." I looked around.

"I was calling you last night, only for your phone to be going to voicemail. Then, this morning, once I finally got you on the phone, you hung up in my face. Where were you?" He shouted.

"I said let's go inside." I rushed up the front steps and pushed past him into the house. I was so irritated that I didn't even take off my shoes, and Lord knows I hated for anyone to walk around my house with shoes on.

"Okay, now where were you, Lovely? I deserve to know!"

"Deserve?" I laughed. "You cannot be serious right now!"

"What is wrong with you?" Glen questioned, looking confused.

"What's wrong with me is that I deserve a man that will love me like I love him, one that will treat me as I treat him, and be faithful to me as I am to him!" He looked at me as if I was boring him.

"Don't start this crying stuff. I know I picked up hours at work, but that doesn't mean I love you any less. Is that what last night was about, you did it for attention? Plan something for next weekend and I'm all yours." He took a seat on the couch as if the problem was fixed.

"You know, Glen, I have been real patient with you. Even nice to your damn momma when the world knows she doesn't deserve it. I put up with her disrespect for the last six years, and not to mention, your snide ass remarks. But you want to know where the bullshit stops?!" I shouted, standing over him.

"Why are you talking like this?" He looked annoyed.

"Because some woman with a baby came to my shop yesterday, looking for you. Well, in her words, our man."

"Huh?" He sat up on the couch.

"Huh my ass. You can hear. She was going to leave her baby with its stepmother because its father, Glen, wasn't answering his phone!" I shouted furiously.

"I don't understand. I don't have a baby."

"So. you don't know a light skin, damn near white, girl, long, red weave, and skinny as hell? The total opposite of me."

"I don't know a lady with that description nor do I have a baby." His face held no emotions.

"Funny that baby looks just like you. I'm not going to sit here going back and forth with you about this. I just want you to get your shit and get the hell out of my house!"

I turned to walk away from him and this whole situation.

"Wait a minute, Lovely." He snatched me back toward him. "I told you I don't know the woman you're talking about, and I don't have a baby. Now you're going to watch your mouth when you talk to me and talk to me with some respect."

Snatching my arm from him, I went in search of my laptop. I may be nice and avoid drama, but I was no fool and wouldn't allow him to play me like I was one. I'd dealt with his mother's disrespect of my weight, skin tone, and my career. She felt I was too fat and black. I was rarely invited to gatherings his mother hosted. Her and the judgmental birds she hung with felt I didn't fit with the image they tried to present. She hated that I owned a salon in the hood, as she called it, and said me being a hairstylist was beneath Glen when Glen only had his job at the bank because of his grandfather. Glen's daddy couldn't even stand her and dipped on her long ago. I never understood how an old ass, single woman living off her daddy's money had room to judge me. Hell, her son moved into my house, and the car he drove was gifted to him by his grandfather. His grandfather was an amazing man and had always treated me with respect. We had lunch together two to three times a month. Before his grandmother passed three months ago, she had me over for lunch once a week, and we did brunch on Sundays. She came to my salon weekly. Seeing as how sweet her parents were, one didn't know where Glen's mother got her snobby attitude.

Locating my laptop, I stomped back to the living room. I found Glen sitting on the couch, sipping a glass of wine, and watching golf without a care in the world. Sitting beside him, I turned on my laptop.

"You say you don't know this woman, but she came into my shop with all this confidence." I pulled up my security feed from the salon. Going to yesterday's feed, I fast forwarded to right before she came in. Placing the laptop in Glen's lap, I hit play. He sat there, barely watching, and it took everything in me not to smack him.

"I told you I don't know her, and I don't have a baby. I do not wish to continue talking about it." He placed the laptop on my lap, not even bothering to finish watching it.

"Oh, don't worry. We don't have to talk about it again. In fact, we won't be speaking ever again." I placed my laptop on the coffee table and stood up. "You're going to get all your shit out of my house. You can go to the baby momma that you claim you don't know or back to your grandparents' house. Where you decide to go, I don't give a damn. You just need to get out of here." I pointed from him to the door.

"You're making me mad."

"I don't give a damn!"

"Would you shut up and stop cursing? What is wrong with you?"

"You're what's wrong with me, sitting here like you didn't screw me over. I want you out, and I want you out tonight!"

"I'm not going anywhere so go lay down or something and get over your little attitude." He stretched out on the couch and started flipping through the channels.

Taking one last look at him, I went into my kitchen, grabbing the box of trash bags, before heading up to my room.

Placing my phone between my ear and shoulder, I started stuffing Glen's items into the bag.

"Hello." Abiri answered the phone, sounding out of breath.

"I want Glen out of my house, and I want him out now!"

"Alright, I'm on my way."

I was working on filling up the third bag when it was snatched out of my hand.

"What are you doing? Have you lost your mind?"

"No, but you have!"

"You have no right messing with my things."

"Glen, I'm not going to go back and forth with you. I want you out. There is nothing else that needs to be said."

"What has gotten into you? I bet it was that wild friend of yours."

"The fact that your baby momma stepped foot in my salon. Then you're trying to play me for a fool."

"I told you I don't know that woman." He shouted, dropping the bag and walking up on me.

"Aye, I know you better lower your voice and take a few steps back." My cousin spoke from the doorway.

"What are you doing in my house?" Glen had the nerve to question.

"Lovely's name on the deed, and you have overstayed your welcome. She asked you to get out, and now, I'm telling you to get the fuck out."

"This is between Lovely and I."

"No, this is between you and I. Lovely asked you to leave, and I'm here to make sure of it. Now grab the bags and whatever you don't have, too bad!" Abiri spoke, stepping into my room and leaning against the dresser.

Glen looked between Abiri and I, it was evident that he didn't really want to leave.

"You're making a big mistake. You belong to me!" He practically spit from his mouth.

"She doesn't belong to anyone." Abiri spoke.

"You'll be crawling back to me, begging me to come back. Who will want you besides me?"

"I can think of one man in particular that will want her. That will actually treat her like she deserves to be treated." Wise spoke from my doorway. I didn't even notice that she was here.

"You probably filled her head with the lies about me. I never liked you and told her to stop hanging out with you!" Glen yelled at Wise. I could see the spit flying from his mouth.

"Alright, that's enough. You have to go. Your shit will be sent to your mother's crib!" Abiri grabbed Glen by the back of his neck and dragged him out of my room.

Wise and I followed behind Abiri as he dragged Glen down the stairs and threw him out onto the front porch before slamming the door. "We are bagging all his shit tonight and getting it out of here. He doesn't need a reason to come back!" He instructed before heading back upstairs.

"Where are his keys and phone? I'll take care of those for you." Wise volunteered.

I scanned the living room for his keys and phone as Glen banged on my front door, screaming threats.

"He normally puts them on this table." I stood in front of the coffee table.

"Shhh, you hear that?" Wise started tossing the pillows on my couch.

Taking a moment, I heard a buzzing sound. I lifted the couch cushion that I was standing in front of. I not only found Glen's phone but another small phone that was buzzing.

"Hello." Wise quickly snatched the phone up and answered.

"Who is this, and where is Glen?" That same annoying voice from my salon yelled from the other end of the phone.

Snatching the phone from Wise, I stomped to the front door, snatching the door open. Glen tumbled inside, falling flat on his face.

"The same woman you didn't claim to know is calling a phone I knew nothing about." I spoke, looking down at him. "Please get up and leave my residence." I dropped his phone, not caring if it landed on him or the ground.

"Lovely, you are making a big mistake!"

"The mistake was even giving you a chance." Wise spoke over my back.

"I wish you would shut your mouth." He spoke while getting up.

"I wish, I wish." Wise sang, stepping around me. "We have some cleansing to do or else I would entertain you. But not tonight. How about you handle that though?" She pointed at his phone that he never hung up. She tossed both his keys and other cell phone at him before slamming the door in his face.

The three of us got to work bagging Glen's remaining belongings. It definitely didn't go unnoticed that I didn't call Wise over, but I would let the two of them do whatever they were doing in peace. When they were ready to tell me the obvious, I would be waiting and welcoming.

Chapter 2

Glen

"How could you let this happen, Glen? You're ruining everything!" My mother paced back and forth after I explained to her about mine and Lovely's break up.

"It wasn't me. It was Sasha." I plopped down on the couch.

"Sasha? I told you to leave that girl alone. What does she have to do with anything?"

"She went to Lovely's shop, and she had the baby with her."

My mother stopped pacing and gave me the most hateful look.

"I told you that girl wasn't worth the trouble that she could possibly create. Now look at you. You fathered a baby with a money-grubbing whore."

"Well, if you would have just watched the baby like I asked, none of this would have happened."

"I raised my child, so I will not be watching yours."

"You didn't raise me. My grandmother did. You know the woman you hated so much?"

"How dare you talk to me like that?!" My mother snapped, slapping me across the face before storming off.

It had been almost three weeks since Lovely put me out. I had been dodging my mother, but she caught me as I pulled up to my grandparents' house to grab some more clothes. She had been blowing my phone up and leaving me angry voice messages. When I left Lovely's house that night, I went and stayed with my snow bunny. I could have come home and faced my mother sooner but would have also risked my grandfather finding out. A lecture from my grandfather, on top of my mother's bitching, was something I didn't need right now. I definitely couldn't risk him finding out about my baby right now with the recent passing of my grandmother and him on my back about doing better in life. I needed a relief from everything - my mother, grandfather, Sasha, and even Lovely. If my grandfather found out about the baby, and the mess I'd made of my relationship with Lovely, he would surely be disappointed in me. But he would disown me if he knew the things I had been involved in lately. Gwen may have birthed me, but it was my grandparents that raised me. Gwen made it clear that she never wanted kids but that she kept me because of who my father was. Well, the man that she thought was my father but she told me out of her own mouth that when she birthed me, she knew there was no way that he could be my father. She literally dropped me off to my grandparents once we were released from the hospital. She went on to live her life as if I didn't exist until she had to come crawling back to her parents because her life was so screwed up.

Imagine you living in the main house with your grandparents while the woman that birthed you lived right out back. She would walk past you daily, most times not uttering a word, and you crying to your grandmother because you didn't know what you did to make her hate you besides being born. Then, your grandmother, being the loving, amazing woman that she was, was there every time to hold you and tell you continuously that your mother did love you. She just had her struggles in life. Although she was screwed up, I loved her and would go out of my way to seek her attention and approval.

Grabbing my keys off the mantle, I rushed out of the guest house, across the yard, and to the front house. I had to fix things with Lovely. I would not let Sasha ruin my plans with Lovely.

"Glen, Glen, where are you?" I heard my grandfather shouting as soon as I stepped into the main house.

"Pops!" I shouted back, making my way from the back porch and through the kitchen.

"Hurry up and get your ass in here!"

The anger in his voice couldn't be missed. Entering the living room, I stopped at the sight of Sasha and the baby in its car seat at her feet.

"What the fuck is this?" My grandfather stood there with his face twisted up and pointing his cigar between Sasha and the baby.

"Pops."

"Don't open your mouth if you're not about to explain this girl and child."

"My child's name is Glen Aiden James Jr." Sasha smacked her lips.

"You know you have done a lot of fucked up things in life. But to cheat on a beautiful woman with the likes of this."

"Beautiful? Please, you can't be talking about that whale." Sasha laughed.

"A whore and dumb one at that is a terrible combination."

"Excuse you, Glen. Are you going to just stand there and let him talk to me like this?"

"You are standing in my home, and I will talk to you as I see fit."

"Your home? Glen, you told me this was your home and that your grandfather lived with you because you took care of him."

"See, this is what happens when you listen to anything a man tells you, just because you think he has money. You end up standing here looking dumb and with a baby that you think is named after its father. Glen couldn't take care of me, even if I gave him all of my money and instructions. In fact, let's be honest. I take care of Glen. He works for me. Well, he barely does that. His middle name isn't Aiden and last name definitely isn't

James."

"What, Glen, you lied to me about this being your house?"

"Get rid of her and meet me in my office." My grandfather walked off, shaking his head.

"What are you doing here?" I turned to Sasha once my grandfather was no longer in the room.

"I've been calling you, and you have not been answering my calls. I went by the Beverly Hills police station and learned that a Glen doesn't work there. What the hell is wrong with you, Glen?"

"Look, I have a lot going on right now. You should have never gone to Lovely's shop nor just popped up here. You have to go." I grabbed her arm, picked up the car seat, and ushered her to the front door.

"What the hell are you doing?" She tried to pull her arm from my grip.

"I will call you when I can, but you have to go." I placed the car seat on the floor, opened the front door, and pushed her out. I sat the car seat outside of the front door.

"Glen, you got me fucked up!" Sasha shouted as I closed the door in her face.

She banged on the door as I made my way to my grandfather's office. I stood outside the door, dreading the lecture he was surely about to give me. While my grandmother was always so understanding and loving, my grandfather showed me tough love and never sugarcoated things with me. Well, with anyone really. He had always been an honest and straightforward person. Taking a few deep breaths and rubbing my sweaty palms down my pants, I pushed the bell. His office was soundproof and equipped with video surveillance. He had always been a bit of a paranoid man. I heard the click that signaled that he had unlocked the door. Pushing it open, I stepped inside and stood by the door.

"Hey, Pops."

"Close the door and have a seat." He sat at his desk with some papers in his hand.

I pushed the door closed and took my time walking over to his desk and sitting in one of the chairs that was positioned in front of his desk. The whole time, he peered at me over his glasses.

He placed the papers he was holding in an envelope and into the drawer of his desk. He took his glasses off and rubbed his eyes while letting out a deep sigh.

"I question myself everyday where I went wrong. For your mother to have pushed you out, and your grandmother and I to have raised you, you are turning out to be just like her."

"Pops..."

He raised his hand, cutting me off. He picked up his phone. "Mary, can you please tell Gwen to come to my office immediately?" He ended the call after a brief pause.

"You are selfish and always have been. I don't know if this is some only child syndrome or the fact my wife coddled you at times, mainly those times you would get in your feelings about a woman that wouldn't so much as tell you hi. Now, it's fucked up how you let Gwen talk to your woman and mistreat her. But to go out and cheat on her and make a baby on her with trash is some shit that I can't make sense of. See, Lovely is a lot like my late wife whereas what just stood in my living room is a lot like Gwen. I mean, I know you have mommy issues but to lay with someone like her. You need help, but you won't get that help on my dime." He pounded his fist on the table.

"Pops..."

"You and Gwen have thirty days to find yourselves a new place of residence. This gravy train has made it to its final station."

"Wait, what? Is this because I told Sasha this is my house? Pops, I didn't mean nothing by it."

"No, this is because I'm tired of carrying the two of you. Your mother thinks life just consists of laying around, not working, having lunch and cocktails with her friends whenever she feels like, spa days, and weekly trips to the hair salon at 51 on my dime. Then you, you're supposed to work 9 a.m. to 2 p.m.,

Monday through Friday, but you come to work when you feel like it. You mistreat my other employees. So, effective immediately, you're fired!"

"Wait, Pops, you can't do that!" I jumped up from my chair.

"What the fuck you want to do?" He stood from his chair as the low sound of a bell floated through his office.

He pressed a button on the keypad, making his dark computer screen come alive. He looked at the monitor as he reached under his desk. My mother stepped through his office door a moment later as he still focused on his screen.

"Yes, Dad, you wanted to see me?" She stayed planted by his door.

He looked at her briefly before focusing back on his computer screen.

"That girl is still on my porch with that baby." He turned the monitor so that I could see that Sasha was indeed still there. The baby was still in front of the door where I placed it while Sasha sat in my granny's rocking chair, rocking back and forth, while smoking a cigarette and on the phone.

"What's going on in here?"

"Close my door and come have a seat."

She closed the door and came over, sitting in the chair on my left.

"Are you going to sit back down, or do you want me to remind you of how soft you are?" He looked me up and down.

"What's going on with you two?"

I slowly sat down, not even responding to my mother.

"Now, I just explained to Glen..." He took his seat. "The two of you are officially being notified that you have until November 1st to find somewhere else to stay. Today is August 17th, so that gives you a little over sixty days to make arrangements."

"What?" My mother leaned forward in her seat.

"No more spa days, salon days, treating your friends to drinks on me. I hope you have been saving money while you've been living here rent free."

"Dad!" My mother shrieked. "Where do you expect me to go? How do you expect me to survive?"

"I don't know. You are grown. Maybe you and your son can get a place together. Get a job and earn your living. Perhaps you can finally be a mother."

"Dad, you're talking nonsense. Why should I live somewhere else when you have all this house?"

"I guess why should you get a job and earn your own money when I am well off, right?"

"Well, yes."

I looked over at my mother and thought about how self-centered and selfish she was.

I didn't know about her, but I had a little money put away and a place to stay.

"I blame myself, just as much as your mother, for the way you turned out, Gwen. Then, I tried to do better and be a little harder on you, Glen. I tried to show you a good work ethic, but apparently, I still didn't do my best. You don't do anything with your life, Gwen, but walk around as if the world owes you something. Your mother cooked, cleaned, and even though she didn't work full time, she didn't just sit around doing nothing nor did she just depend on me financially even though I wanted her to relax and let me take care of everything. But you didn't pick up any of our traits. Then you, Glen, mistreating a beautiful girl, you barely want to work, and you have some girl popping up at my house. Quite frankly, I'm tired. I worked too hard to let you two leeches live off me." My grandfather leaned back in his chair and sighed.

"This is all your fault." My mother turned in her seat and yelled at me. "You can't do anything right. You are always ruining things. You just couldn't stick to the plan." My mother quickly closed her mouth as her eyes widened.

"What plan would that be, Gwen?" My grandfather sat up straight in his chair.

"Nothing!" My mother answered my grandfather, never taking her eyes off me.

"Gwen, since a child, you have always been sneaky, manipulative, self-centered, selfish, and always out for gain. Whatever you have going on, don't pull this boy down that never ending black tunnel with you."

Snapping her neck in his direction, I just knew her neck had to hurt.

"As my father, you are supposed to always support me, but you just sat here and said you're putting me out. Then, you turn around and call me selfish. Who is really being selfish? I'm your only child. How can you just try to toss me to the side?"

"Gwen, you're grown as hell. You talk about me tossing you to the side, but when is Glen's birthday? When is the last time you told your son you love him if ever? Gwen, I'm not your mother, and you have never known me to be light about what I say to you since the time you started thinking you were grown. Your mother may have been gentle with you, but that's just the type of person she was with everyone. But Gwen, I know what you're trying to do right now. You're trying to guilt trip someone. But dear, I'm snatching that Persian rug from under you, this nice life that you don't appreciate and feel that, just because I'm your father, I'm supposed to give your grown ass."

My mother quickly hopped out of her chair, causing it to crash to the ground, and stormed out of the office. My grandfather sat there, staring at the door. He finally looked in my direction.

"Glen, whatever your mother has going on, don't let her bring you down with her. Yes, you screw up and take things for granted, but it is not too late to make changes in your life for the better." He looked at his computer screen. "Now, I'm assuming you know that child is yours one hundred percent." He never took his eyes off the screen.

"Yes, I had a DNA test performed."

"Don't be your mother." He looked at me. "Take care of your child and do better. You will not learn nor grow in life if I keep handing you things. The mistake we made with your mother..." He reached in his drawer, pulling an envelope from it and tossing it to me. "That is $50,000. Don't spend it all at once. I guess we can say your sixty-day timeframe starts now. Go tend to your child and get the mother off my porch." He looked at his computer screen once before shutting it down.

Standing up, he grabbed his phone and keys. I stood as well and headed out of his office. I headed to my room to put this money away.

Chapter 3

Craft

I was sitting in my office, going over this week's schedule and inventory for my speed dating event tomorrow night, when my cousin burst in my office.

"What up, young one?"

"I know your mother taught you to knock before entering." I threw a pen at him as he dropped down into the chair in front of my desk.

"Man, you knew I was coming. You buzzed me in. So, don't start your shit today." He tossed the envelope in his hand on my desk before kicking his feet up.

"You disrespectful as fuck." I grabbed the envelope and pulled the papers out.

"Respect your elders." He laughed.

"Aye, what's up with your brother? He's been a little snappy lately, and he definitely was sloppy on the field Friday."

"Just like you, a chick got his head spinning."

I placed the papers down. I was going over to give my cousin my undivided attention.

"Man, don't nobody have my head spinning. I can admit I'm very intrigued, but I'm focused."

"Yeah, I hear you."

"You don't have something else you can be doing right now?"

"Nah, but you know who your girl is, right?" He chuckled.

Ignoring him, I went back to reading the papers. I now knew that the beauty from the club looked familiar, but I just couldn't place where from. "Lovely," I recited her name, and a lovely sight she was, from her skin, that was the color of a Hershey bar that I just wanted to lick, the beautiful voice that I wanted to speak my name, the body that I just wanted to run my fingers against every inch of her frame, to that beautiful smile that I wouldn't mind keeping on her face.

"You see who she is related to?"

Dropping the papers, I just stared at him for a moment.

"You gone let me read, or do you prefer to just tell me everything?"

"I mean, I could tell you the little that I know, but you got it."

"Well, silence, damn." I picked up the papers and continued reading, learning everything I needed to know about my Lovely. The fact that I did business with her family was even better, and the one person that I thought was her man a couple years ago was really her cousin. I looked at Honor, who was cheesing from ear to ear.

"What the fuck you smiling so hard for?"

"Abiri gone fuck you up about his cousin."

"Abiri ain't gone do shit!"

"I bet old man Nelson can knock you on your ass." He laughed.

I leaned over and knocked his feet off my desk.

"You always wanted to be his grandson." He laughed.

"Shut the fuck up!"

"What? You're in the family now." He shrugged.

"Anyways, I have two speed dating events scheduled this week, tomorrow night and Sunday. I will need you at Sheetz Saturday and Sunday. Definitely Saturday if anything. I'm expecting a large crowd. I had to turn many people away already, just waiting on test results," I spoke, placing the papers back in the folder and securing them inside my desk.

"Damn, well, I'm there both days."

"Also, we will have a few high-profile clients. So, everyone needs to be on point. Make sure all cellphones are checked in at the door before entrance. I don't know who was covering the door the last time, but a phone made it on the floor."

"On it."

"If everything is going well with your business, then we are good."

"Yeah, everything is good. Although Orion has been asking to get in the ring."

"No." I stood, grabbing my suit jacket, keys, and phone.

"Well, you're going to have to talk to him about your decision." Honor stood, releasing a sigh.

"I don't have to explain shit to him. The answer is no. We allowed him once. My auntie not about to stress me because you are scared of your little brother. But if he has a problem with my answer, the only way we are talking about it is if he gets in the ring with me."

"Man, you would think that you and Orion were brothers instead of him and I. The two of you are just alike." Honor chuckled.

"That's my little nigga, but he need to focus on school and football. I will holla at him one of these days, but for now, I need to get the girls. We have some places to be and people to see."

"I'm sure I know where your dapper ass is going. Don't be trying to use my nieces to get pussy."

"I don't have to use them for nothing. I'm just trying to scope out the scene." Honor and I left my office, going our separate ways.

At twenty-seven, I ran lucrative businesses and had two beautiful beings depending on me, but I didn't have the one yet.

"Hey, Uncle Craft." My niece, Peace, meekly spoke, climbing in the car.

"Hey, P. Where is Skylar?"

I looked back at her, and she just shrugged her shoulders.

"She should have been out thirty minutes ago." I checked

my watch.

"I don't know." She shrugged her shoulders once more.

"Alright, let's go inside this school." I left my car parked right in the pickup line. They wanted to inconvenience me today. I would inconvenience them.

"Hey, you can't park there." A teacher yelled at my back.

Ignoring her, I grabbed Peace and proceeded inside the school. Checking my daughter's class first and finding it empty, I made my way to the main office.

"Hello. I'm trying to find my daughter, Skylar Carter. She wasn't outside for pickup." I spoke, approaching the counter.

"Um, hello. Yes, she is in the principal office." The lady spoke, never looking up from her computer.

"You are typing on that computer and haven't even verified who I am, but you're giving out information about a student with no problem. Add the fact that no one thought to call me to tell me my daughter was in the office." I smacked my hand on the counter.

"Hello, Mr. Carter. Please step into my office." The principal spoke from her doorway.

"Next time, how about getting up out of your seat and verifying I'm the parent? I could have been anybody." I threw over my shoulder while heading to the principal's office with Peace right behind me.

Stepping into the office, my eye started twitching, and sweat started forming above my top lip. I was heated, looking at my daughter with one of her ponytails missing.

"Hey, Daddy!" She smiled brightly at me.

"Mr. Carter, there was an incident today. This is only the second week of school, and I do not wish to have a repeat of first grade."

I took a look around the office. "Was she involved in this incident by herself?"

"Excuse me?"

"My daughter is in your office, holding one of her ponytails in her hand, with a swollen lip. Now unless she had some freak accident, why is she the only child in here?"

"Well, the other parents were notified, and they already picked their children up."

"I was taught to respect my elders, but you are about to make me disrespect you."

I turned my attention to my daughter because I was seconds away from flipping the principal's desk over. "Baby, what happened?" I kneeled before her.

"Well, we were doing art time in class after lunch, and that boy, Jacob, cut my ponytail. When I told the teacher, she told me to go back to my seat. So, I did what you taught me, and I beat him up." She said the last part so proudly.

"Good job, baby. Daddy is proud of you!" I kissed her forehead.

"Mr. Carter, we do not condone fighting."

"That little boy deserved to get his ass whooped." I stood up and spun around so fast. "My daughter is missing a damn ponytail. She is telling me that this happened over two hours ago, and no one notified me."

"Daddy, that's not all." Skylar tugged on my pants.

"What happened, baby?" I took a moment to look at the principal before giving my daughter my full attention.

"Well, his sister, Jasmin, is in the class too. While I was beating Jacob up, she jumped in."

"So, you're telling me that not only did a little boy cut her hair, but another student jumped on my daughter too?" I was so mad I could put my hands on this lady.

"Mr. Carter, I spoke with the other students' parents. They will be suspended for two days along with Skylar." She sat behind her desk with her nose turned up.

"So, you had no problem calling the other parents and speaking with them, but you couldn't give me the same respect?" I spoke, pulling my jacket off because I was getting so hot.

"Mr. Carter, you have shown before that you do not do well with the other parents." She spoke, looking like she didn't care for this meeting.

"That's okay. I'll be speaking with my lawyer. I'll make sure to knock you off your high horse and out of your current position."

"That will not be necessary. I believe I have given each student a fair enough punishment."

"Come on, Skylar and Peace." I turned and reached out a hand to each of them. "Oh, don't worry. They won't be back." I spoke, heading out the door, not even granting her the respect of facing her. My daughter had dealt with constant bullying, especially by the little boy, Jacob. For these kids to only be seven years old, they could be so cruel at times.

Leaving the school, I took my two little ladies to get some wings. It was unfortunate my baby lost her hair, but now, I wouldn't look like a stalker dropping by Lovely's shop.

"Where are we going, Daddy?" Skylar, the inquisitive and talkative one of the two, questioned.

"I'm taking you two to visit a friend of mine. We're going to see what she can do about that hair of yours." I glanced in my rearview mirror at the two of them.

I was a single dad to two little queens, and most days, I still felt like I didn't know what I was doing. At eight and seven, you would think I had this fatherhood thing down pat, but the way my aunt fussed at me, I knew I needed to take any and all classes available. I could only do a simple ponytail, not that I hadn't tried other styles. Skylar wore this one outfit every week - overall shorts, this princess t-shirt with a hood, and rain boots. I really would be glad when she grew out of it. Peace was simple - sweatsuits and Jordans. Peace was quiet and barely talked most days. Skylar talked enough for the both of them. She literally spoke for Peace.

My Aunt Marie and her husband, David, raised my sister, Sky, and I since she was twelve and I was seven. So, I really thought of Honor and Orion as more of my brothers than my cousins. My mom loved a nigga more than she loved herself. She was pregnant with me and legit let a nigga beat me out of her. For years, we witnessed and experienced the abuse on many occasions. Then, one night, her screams suddenly went silent. After not eating for two days and our parents never coming out of their room, my sister and I took the long walk from our two-bedroom apartment in Imperial Courts Housing Projects to our aunt's house located near Acacia and Compton Boulevard. You could only imagine how angry she was at not only the condition we were in when we showed up at her home but also at the fact that we walked to her home by ourselves. That was a good distance for two kids, and we were showing up to her house at night. After cleaning and feeding us, her and David drove us back home. David kicked in the bedroom door to find my dad lying with my mother's lifeless body. I remembered my sister crying, David beating my father, and my aunt crying while cradling my mother's body. I didn't remember when the police showed up or any of us leaving the house.

Unfortunately, my sister followed in my mother's footsteps. I wasn't able to save her, but I made sure the nigga wished he kept his hands to himself. Before I beat him like he did my sister and buried him alive, I made sure he watched the three people he loved the most beat him to hell.

Peace had been in my care since she was three months old once she was finally released from the hospital. Then, Skylar's momma dropped her off the day after her first birthday and dropped off the face of the earth. With Skylar, she wasn't missing much because her momma was something to do when there was nothing to do. At times, I really hated that my girls didn't have a proper mother figure. They had Aunt Marie, but I just wished at times they had a woman in the house.

"Daddy, where are we?" Skylar pulled me from my thoughts as we pulled in front of Lovely's shop.

"I told you to see my friend about your hair." I turned and faced the two of them as I spoke. "We will get you in a chair too, Peace, my little g, if that's cool with you?"

In her normal fashion, she simply nodded her head.

"Alright, make sure you ladies get all your trash and let's head in." I hopped out, making my way to the back passenger door and opening the door.

Lovely

"Who is that fine man right there?" one of my stylists, Joyce, yelled out.

"Fine and wearing the hell out of that suit." Another stylist, Jasmine, spoke.

Looking out the window, I instantly got hot. The man that had found his way into my dreams every night was helping two little girls out of the back of his truck. I watched his every move until he was standing in front of the receptionist booth, holding each of the girls' hands. Gorgeous gave him her normal greeting, but his eyes roamed the shop until they landed on me. I watched his lips move until they formed a smile. Then, his head tilted in my direction before guiding the two cuties in my direction.

"Wait, what happened to that baby hair?" Wise broke me from my trance.

"This boy at school cut it." The little girl spoke with a pout while dangling a piece of the ponytail in her hand.

"Oh. hell no! Where is his little ass at?" Wise questioned, grabbing her keys.

"It's okay. I beat him and his sister up." She boasted with the biggest smile on her face.

"Oh, they are about to get a double beat up. Come on, Gorgeous. We have to go see some kids about my friend." Wise smiled while the two little girls giggled.

"Wise, cut it out. You are not about to go fight no kids. Although we know you would probably really try to." I made my way over to the two little beauties.

I squatted to get eye level with the two of them. "Hello, ladies. I'm Lovely, and you are?"

"I'm Skylar!" The one with the missing ponytail spoke. "This is my cousin."

"Peace. My name is Peace." She spoke meekly.

I shook both their hands. "I'm assuming you're here to get a cute hairstyle?"

"Yes, my daddy said he will see if he can get us in a chair, but I don't really need my hair done because I got suspended." Skylar spoke, looking between her father and I.

"Suspended?" Wise shouted. "Oh, hell nah! I may not be able to fight a kid, but whoever suspended you gone have to see me."

"The principal!" Skylar shouted, clearly loving Wise's antics.

"You wild, but I may need you to spin the block with me on the principal."

"Skylar, baby, don't listen to Wise. Wise, please stop cursing in front of these babies and see what type of hairstyle little Ms. Peace would like. Why don't you come with me, so we can send you back to school looking fabulous?" I grabbed Skylar's hand. "You, Dad, you can have a seat in the chair next to my booth or on the front couch." I pointed between the two.

Without a word, he made his way to the chair by my booth. Skylar and I followed right behind him.

"Okay, Ms. Skylar, do you have a style in mind?" I asked, placing her in my chair.

"I don't know. My daddy normally tells that other girl to braid my hair back, but I didn't like going to her."

"Oh, no, why not?"

"She was too busy watching my daddy. She would just be turning my head like this and like this." She demonstrated by moving her hands side to side.

"Oh, really?" I questioned, cutting my eyes at her daddy, who was staring at me.

"Yes, and she braided my hair too tight. My Auntie Marie would just take them down and give me ponytails."

"Oh, okay. Well, how about I braid your hair into two ponytails with some beads? But what I will do is add some hair so that we can make up for what that little boy cut off." I spoke while taking her ponytails down.

"I guess that will be okay. I never had beads before."

"Never? Oh, no. Every little girl should experience beads.

But we're going to wash your hair first." I helped her out of the chair.

"I hope it's not like how my daddy does it. He gets water everywhere."

"I try my best, kid." Her father finally spoke.

"Okay, Dad. We are going to the shampoo room that is right on the other side of this wall." I pointed.

"Craft."

"Excuse me?"

"My name is Craft, Craft Carter."

"Well, Mr. Carter, you are more than welcome to join us. But you are also free to stay right here."

"Craft is fine, and can I stand in the doorway? I want to be able to keep an eye on both my girls."

"You've only kept your eye on one person since you've been here. She definitely isn't one of your girls," Wise sarcastically remarked, causing everyone to laugh.

I cut my eye at Wise before focusing on Craft. "You are more than welcome to stand in the doorway, Mr. Carter."

"Craft, but we'll work on that." He stood from the chair and followed us to the shampoo room while the stylists made a few smart remarks behind our retreating backs.

I placed a booster seat in the chair for the shampoo bowl so that she was sitting high enough that I didn't have to strain my back.

"Alright, are you ready?"

"Yes!" She shook her head while wearing a big smile.

"Alright, let's climb up here." I grabbed her hand and helped her climb into the chair. "Okay, turn around and sit back."

I grabbed all my supplies that I needed, wrapped a towel around her shoulders first, and then dropped a cap over her. I reclined the chair back.

"How do you feel? Are you comfortable?"

"Yes."

I got to work detangling and washing her hair as Wise and Peace stepped into the room. They were stopped by Craft, who whispered something in Wise's ear, causing her eyes to drop to Peace. She nodded her head before guiding Peace to a shampoo bowl. Craft stood in the doorway, watching us intently. I put the conditioner on and sat Skylar under the dryer for ten minutes. Once I rinsed and blow dried her hair, I directed her to my station to braid her up.

"Okay, Dad ,we're finished." I nudged her father, who had fallen asleep in the chair next to my workstation.

"Sorry about that." His eyes popped open, and he looked around.

"That's alright. That chair gets the best of everyone." The shop erupted in laughter. "Okay, tell me how you like your hair." I turned Skylar to the mirror.

"I love it!" She sang. "Look, Daddy, look how pretty it is." She excitedly jumped from my chair.

"Be careful, sweetie!"

"I got this, Lovely. I jump off stuff all the time." She smiled up at me. "Daddy, do you like my hair?"

"Well, let me get a good look at you. Do your princess spin." He grabbed her hand, spinning her around. "You're beautiful, baby girl. I think I need to go and buy you and Peace some princess dresses. I don't think sweatsuits will go with your hairstyles." He spoke, looking between the two of them.

"A princess dress? Really, Daddy?"

"Okay, maybe not a princess dress. Maybe a couple of those girly outfits that Aunt Marie suggested that I get the two of you. Maybe we can get Ms. Lovely to help us out with a little shopping tomorrow?" He looked up at me.

"Um, I'm..."

"Please, Ms. Lovely, can you come? My daddy doesn't know what he's doing when we go shopping." Skylar wrapped her arms around me.

"Hey, you've never complained before."

"I don't think that's a good idea, sweetie." I looked down at her while rubbing her back.

"Why not?"

"Lovely, I have given you your space. It's time for you to come to your senses." Glen barged into my shop.

"Glen, you need to leave my place of business." I placed Skylar behind me.

"No, I've given you your space for a couple of days. You're going to talk to me. I am sick of this shit." He stomped toward me.

"She asked you to leave." Craft stepped in front of me.

"Who are you?"

"None of your concern but I do recall that she asked you to leave."

"This is my fiancé so step out of the way."

"Your fiancé, huh?" Craft questioned, looking over his shoulder at me.

"We're not together anymore." I answered Craft.

"Who is this guy, Lovely? Have you been cheating on me with him?" Glen questioned.

"You have a lot of nerve showing up to my shop and questioning me at that!" I attempted to step around Craft, but he stuck his arm out, halting me.

"Who is he?" Glen questioned, looking from me to Craft's arm.

"As I stated before, who I am is of no concern to you, but the lady asked you to leave, and I will see to it that you do."

"This is between me and my fiancé."

"Ex-fiancé." Wise spoke.

"No one is talking to you, ghetto trash!" He whipped around in Wise's direction. "This is all your fault. I told her to stop hanging with you."

He took two steps in Wise's direction before Craft snatched him up by the back of his shirt and marched him to the front door that Gorgeous was conveniently holding open. He literally tossed Glen on his ass. Bending down, he said something to Glen. Whatever was said had Glen up and running.

"So, Wise?" Craft stepped back into the shop like nothing

had happened.

"Yes."

"How much do I owe you?" he questioned, pulling money from his pocket.

"75."

"Keep the change." He placed some bills in her hand before making his way to me.

"How much do I owe you, Ms. Lovely?" He spoke, stopping in front of me.

"75 as well."

"I hope that you will take us up on the offer of joining us tomorrow for a little shopping. I know it will make my girls' day." He spoke, placing three one-hundred-dollar bills in my hand.

"This is too much." I tried giving him two back.

"How about you put your number in my phone, so I can call to set up their next appointment or maybe a date for the two of us?" He pulled his phone out.

"Appointment, yes. Date, no." I put my number in his phone and handed it back to him. "I'll see you two beauties another time." I hugged both Skylar and Peace.

Chapter 4

Craft

"Aye, you still pouting about getting turned down a couple of weeks back?" Honor barged into my office.

"You still acting like your momma didn't raise you right?"

"Oh, yeah, your feelings are still hurt."

"Nigga, I'm straight. What does your annoying ass want?" I slid the papers I was going over to the side.

"I came up here to put a smile on your face. But I think I'd rather see you sweat."

"What is your goofy ass talking about?"

"Nothing. I have to get back downstairs to make sure none of these dudes get out of hand with the beautiful ladies." He got up, walking over and standing by the door with this big ass smile on his face.

"Nah, what did you come up here for?"

"Oh, nothing, never mind."

"Your goofy ass is always on some bullshit. I thought you and your boy, Abiri, had business to take care of." I hopped up quickly, threw on my suit jacket, and grabbed my cell phone and keys.

"I do, but we pushed it back. I wanted to make your day, princess." He walked out of my office. Closing and locking the door, I quickly made my way downstairs to see what Honor was up to.

"Table six." Honor spoke as soon as my foot hit the last

step.

I looked around in confusion until my eyes landed on her. My tie suddenly felt a little tight, and I felt like I should have left my suit jacket behind.

"What is she doing here? I don't remember her name being on this list."

"I remember her friend, Wise's name being on the list."

"I don't even remember her name being on the list."

"That's because she has your head fucked up. We have had to go behind you and double check the paperwork."

"Man, whatever, but I'll be back." I made my way to her table as a table change was taking place. "My man, find another table." I grabbed the chair that the guy was getting ready to sit in that was across from Lovely.

"We're supposed to go in order." He spoke before turning and facing me. "Um, Mr. Carter."

"I just need the seat. You will be fully refunded." I spoke, easing into the chair.

"Mr. Carter." She greeted me with raised eyebrows.

"Ms. Lovely, how are you tonight?"

"I'm well and you?"

"I would be better if you had replied to my text and joined the girls and I for a little shopping like we had asked you. Also, if you weren't utilizing my speed dating services."

"Oh, so this is your business, huh?" She looked around. "And my business line is just that, for business."

"Alright, I hear you." I responded while placing her name card down, signaling that she was done for the night.

"Why would you do that? The night is just getting started, and I have quite a few more men to talk to. It's bad enough you already ran one off. That could have been my husband." She sat the name card back up.

"See, Lovely, in here," I waved my hand around, "I'm your only option." I took her card with her name printed on it off the holder and placed it in my jacket pocket.

"Trying to bully me won't get you too far."

"I'm not trying to bully you, baby. I'm trying to get to experience you."

"I'm going to head out." She spoke to her friend while grabbing her purse.

"I want to experience kissing those beautiful lips, running my hands from your throat to between those luscious thighs."

She quickly reached over the table and covered my mouth with her hand. I licked her hand, causing her to quickly remove it.

"How about we get out of here, and you join me for dinner?"

She looked between her friend and I a few times while nibbling on her bottom lip, something that I wished I was doing.

"Dinner and no funny business, Mr. Carter."

"Me dining on you definitely wouldn't be a funny situation."

"Craft!" She shrieked.

Shrugging my shoulders, I stood from my seat. "Give me a moment to speak with two individuals."

"No need. We got this. Go ahead before she changes her mind and have you moping around here again." Honor spoke as he stood beside me. "Hello, long time no see." Honor reached his hand in Lovely's direction.

"Hello, yes, I haven't seen you in about a year maybe." She smiled at him.

I smacked his hand down. "Gone somewhere, man."

"My bad!" He raised his hands, backing away. "It was nice seeing you."

"You as well." She smiled.

"Don't be smiling at his ugly ass."

"Don't be jealous, Mr. Carter."

"Jealous?"

"Yes, jealous. He is handsome though." She giggled.

"Keep it up. I'm going to go on your business website and leave some bad reviews."

"You wouldn't dare!"

"Have fun, best friend, and try to do some things that you know I would do."

"Absolutely not, Wise."

"Let's head out." I placed my hand on the dip in her back and guided her to the front door.

"Don't be good!" Wise shouted after us.

I was familiar with Wise from attending the women's kickboxing class that was held at my gym two times a week. It wasn't until she started frequenting my fight nights with Abiri that I formed a friendship with her. Abiri was a friend of Honor's as well as a business partner. Today was Wise's first time here, and I knew this wasn't by chance. Making it to the door, I looked back in her direction. She smiled and winked at me, and I gave her a quick nod and continued out the door.

We made it to my car, and I opened the passenger door and assisted her inside.

"Thank you."

"You're welcome, beautiful." I closed the door, went to the driver's side, and slid in. "Do you have a favorite restaurant or food?"

"I like Maggiano's, and then, I have this little spot in San Pedro that I like to go to."

"So, if you had your pick, which one would you choose tonight?" I started the car.

"Puesta Del Sol. That's the restaurant in San Pedro that I like."

"Cool. San Pedro it is." I eased out of the parking spot.

"I can't wait to get a margarita and their chips and salsa."

I quickly glanced over in her direction before focusing back on the road. "What made you come out to speed dating tonight?"

"Wise. Let her tell it, I need to get out more."

"I thought she had a man. What is she doing dragging you out tonight to speed dating of all places?"

"Yeah, she mentioned this new guy, but I haven't had the pleasure of meeting him yet." She giggled.

"Oh, yeah? Why are you laughing about it?"

"I kind of have an idea, but I'm trying to let my two best friends live."

"Who's your other best friend?"

"My cousin, Abiri."

"Abiri?" Even though I knew everything I needed to know about her, I still wanted to know about her directly from her. "That's crazy. He and my cousin, Honor, kind of got cool from all of us attending old man Nelson's gym. Well, they started hanging out after high school and me being younger, I wasn't allowed to tag along with them. But I'm trying to figure out why I never had the pleasure of meeting you?"

"You were too young to hang with them? How old are you?"

"Twenty-seven."

"Twenty-seven?" Her eyes bucked.

"Yes, twenty-seven. Is that a problem?"

"I'm thirty-one years old, Mr. Craft."

"Thirty-one and fine as ever." I quickly looked over and caught the smile she was trying to bite back. "But yes, I know you're older than me, and it doesn't bother me. Does the age difference bother you?"

"We're just going to have a bite to eat, so it is no big deal."

"So, again, how is it that we're just meeting?"

"You were too young to hang with the big boys, and I wasn't much of the type to hang with the boys."

"Oh, we're taking shots, huh?" I laughed while shaking my head.

"No, little baby." She laughed.

"I'm a fully grown man, but you'll find out."

"Mr. Carter," she sternly said, cracking her window even though the AC was blowing through the car, "so, with our cousins being friends, how is it that I've never met you?"

"We're cousins, but he has his group of friends, and I have mine. We work together and see each other at my aunt's house all the time because, even though we're grown, there's nothing like our place of comfort. Here and there, we might pop out to a club or two. But between being a father and my different business revenues, hanging out isn't a top priority."

"I would say, Mr. Carter, daddy mode does look good on you, besides the suits. I mean, that's the word floating around my salon."

"Thank you, beautiful."

"No, it wasn't me that said it." She quickly backpedaled. She looked at me with bucked eyes.

"I hear you, baby." I winked at her.

"Whatever." She rolled her eyes, smiling. "Um, what is the relationship status between you and your daughters' mother?"

"My daughter and my niece."

"Excuse me?"

"Skylar is my daughter; Peace is my niece. Skylar's mother walked away when she was one, and Peace's mother, my sister, Sky, never had the chance to meet her daughter."

"Oh, I'm so sorry!" She hesitantly placed her hand on my arm that rested on the center console.

"Thank you."

"You're welcome."

We rode in a comfortable silence.

"So, you said you had multiple business revenues. Mind if I inquire?"

"Well, I have Companion, my establishment I just rescued you from."

"Rescued? How do you know my husband wasn't back there?"

"I'm not even going to justify that with an answer. But I also have Match, my boxing gym."

"A boxing gym, huh?"

"I actually took ownership of your grandfather's gym. I just changed the name and tweaked a few things."

"Wow, I haven't been past there in so long."

"Yeah, I hadn't been there for about two years when I walked in on Abiri telling Honor about Mr. Nelson's plans to close shop and sell the building."

"Yeah, I remember my aunts fussed at him for about a year that it was time for him to sit down somewhere. He gave them hell until he finally gave in."

"Yeah, he's a tough man and was always tough on those that needed it. I'm a prime example. He looked out for me and many other young men in the community at a time we needed him the most. If it wasn't for your grandfather, I'm not sure where I would be today."

"I am glad you had him to be there for you. So, was boxing something you were trying to turn into a career or more of just a hobby?"

"I thought I was going to be the next Holyfield. Your grandfather was big on self-discipline and always preached education first. 'Life throws you curveballs. You can have it all figured out, can have the greatest and what you might think is a foolproof plan. But life never goes as we plan.'"

"Yes, that sounds like my grandfather. That is the same thing he instilled in his children and their children."

"Yes, well, I'm thankful. I soaked up everything he taught me, but when my sister passed, that was my..." I took a deep breath, "that was my point of life having other plans. I was nineteen going on twenty, suddenly responsible for two kids, two toddlers. I had already been taking business classes because education was something else your grandfather drilled into me. With the help of my aunt and uncle taking care of the girls, I finished school."

"Yes, my grandfather is an amazing man, and his past mistakes were great lessons. I'm glad my grandfather could be to you what he was to me."

"Thank you."

"Also, it takes an amazing man to detour his dreams and be a father, a single father to two little, beautiful beings. You're an amazing man, Mr. Carter."

"You keep throwing compliments at me, and I may start thinking that you're taking a liking to me."

"Oh, please!" She rolled her eyes as I exited the freeway.

We rode down Gaffey in silence. I was lost in my thoughts about the very thing that Mr. Nelson said life would do.

Lovely

"What? Why are you looking at me like that?" I questioned after he backed into a parking spot and shut the car off.

"You're beautiful. I have a confession. The night at the strip club, I watched you from the moment you stepped in. You were enjoying yourself with your friend, not to mention throwing that big ass."

"Oh, my God." I cupped my hands over my face, embarrassed.

"Nothing to be embarrassed about." He removed my hands.

"I can't believe you saw me like that. That's not me."

"Well, we can blame that night on the liquor, but when you shake that ass on me, there won't be any liquor in your system." He slid out of the car with his words lingering in the air.

Coming around to my side of the car and opening the door, he reached his hand out in front of me. Grabbing a hold of it, he assisted me out of the car.

"What did you mean by that?"

"By what?"

"What did you say before you got out of the car?"

"All I said was are you ready to eat?" He winked at me before placing his hand on my lower back, prompting me to walk.

"Hello, how many are in your party tonight?" The hostess greeted us.

"Just two."

"Oh, hey, Lovely." The waitress, Erica, greeted as she grabbed two menus before leading us to our table. "Here you are and I hope everything is to your liking tonight. Enjoy." She placed the menus on the table once we were seated.

"I'll give you a moment to look over the menu because I

want your undivided attention."

"Oh, I know what I want so go ahead."

"Well, what do you recommend?"

Sitting across from him, I felt so nervous. He was so beautiful - if that was even a way to describe a man. He had a caramel skin tone and dimples that were permanently dimpling without him even smiling. Then, his hair was fine, and the way his waves dipped, I was sure if I could shrink myself and sit on them, I'd be going up and down. The night I saw him in the club, I thought he was so handsome but sitting in front of him now, even with a suit on that I was sure was tailored to fit his body, I just wanted to reach out and caress him.

"You know we can skip dinner and head to my place, but I was trying to take things slow and be a gentleman. But the way you're over there nibbling your lips while raking your eyes over me, I don't know if I should feel exposed or aroused."

"Huh?" I snapped from my thoughts.

"I see you appreciate what you see, as do I. But Lovely, you can't look at me the way you were just looking at me, or I'm going to have to take things to third base a lot sooner. In which I definitely doubt you're ready for that."

"Wait, what? I wasn't..."

"It's okay. Now are you going to tell me what you normally order, or do we need to call it a night, so I can feast on what it is that I really want?"

"Oh," was my only response as my palms got sweaty, and my breathing became labored. I never had someone be so forward with me. I mean, I'd only had two sexual partners, and Glen was nothing like Craft. Even after as long as we'd been together, he still beat around the bush when it was time to have sex. It was like I always had to be the aggressor and initiate sex with him.

"So, what's good here?"

I watched him swipe his tongue across his lips.

"Um, I normally get the a la carte. The three tacos and a beef enchilada."

"Have you tried anything else on the menu?"

"I had the lobster enchiladas once before. But I'm a creature of habit, so I tend to stick to what I know."

"Hello, I have some fresh chips and salsa here." The waitress placed the two dishes on the table. "Can I get you started with anything to drink?"

"Yes, can I get a Pepsi as well as a mango margarita blended with nothing around the rim, but can I get Hennessy instead of tequila as my liquor in my margarita?"

"Okay, and you, sir?"

"Hennessy, huh?" He looked at me before focusing back on the waitress. "Let me get a double shot of Hennessy and do you have lemonade? I'm not much of a soda drinker."

"Yes, we have lemonade, but we also have our watermelon, cucumber, pineapple, or mango agua frescas flavors as well as horchata."

"I'll try the watermelon agua fresca."

"Great choice. Do you need more time for your food choice, or are you ready?"

"A little more time please. This is his first time here."

"Okay, no problem. I'll be back shortly with your drinks." She scurried away.

"How about me order a few different things and we just share?" Craft suggested while picking his menu back up.

"Sure, I'm cool with that as long as we get some of the street tacos."

"Most definitely. I know I want the wings. You almost can't go wrong with wings." He chuckled.

"I've had their wings before, no complaints. How about we get the fiesta platter as well?"

"Alright, so a couple of the street tacos, wings, and fiesta platter?"

"Yes, Mr. Carter." I smirked.

"You are going to call me Craft yet."

"What if I like calling you Mr. Carter?"

"I can bet you'll love calling me Craft even more, just wait on it."

"Okay, here is your Pepsi and your watermelon agua fresca. Your drinks from the bar should be over soon. Have you had a chance to look over the menu?" She placed our drinks before us.

"Yes, we will like an order of the buffalo wings, the fiesta platter, but are we able to get chicken added to the nachos?" Craft questioned while reciting our order.

"Yes, of course. Will there be anything else?"

"Yes, we will also like the three carne asada tacos, and can I please get the red sauce on the side?" I requested.

"Yes, no problem. If that will be all, I will get these menus out of your way and put your order in." She grabbed the menus and made her way to the kitchen.

"So, Mr. Carter, while you're here with me, where are the two little ladies in your life?"

"With my aunt."

"Are there any women in your life romantically?"

Before he could answer, our drinks from the bar were being placed at the table.

"Here you are, one double shot of Hennessy for you, sir, and for my friend, the mango Hennessy margarita." One of the bartenders, Franco, greeted.

"Thank you, Franco."

"You are welcome. Let us know if you need anything else."

"Your friend, huh?" Craft questioned as Franco walked away.

"I told you I like this place, and I practically get the same thing every time."

"I have to watch you."

"What did I do?"

"You're beautiful. That's all."

"So, back to the question, Mister. Are you romantically involved with anyone at the moment?"

"No, I'm not."

"So, no woman thinks she has claims to you, right?" I took

a sip of my drink.

"No, not at all." He grabbed his drink and drank it in two swigs. "So, tell me, is the salon your only business?"

"Well, no. I also own the barbershop that's just down the street from my salon, and I have a few rental properties."

"Businesswoman. Okay, I like that. As much as I frequent the barbershop, I always thought Sean owned it."

"You're not the only one." She giggled.

"So, tell me what do you like to do for fun?"

"I'm a homebody for the most part. If I'm not at my shop, I'm home. Partying isn't my thing."

"With a friend like Wise, how does that work?"

"Well, you see she had me out that night you came to my rescue. So here and there, I'll indulge in her activities."

"Well, I guess it's my turn to get you out of the house sometimes?"

"We will see how tonight goes." I grabbed my drink and resumed drinking it while he watched me intensely. We sat in a comfortable silence while I finished my drink just as the waitress sat our food before us.

"Alright, it smells good and looks good." Craft grabbed the plate of wings.

"Can we have an extra side of red salsa please?"

"Sure, would you like anything else?"

"Yes, can we each get another drink from the bar?"

"Yes, of course. Will it be the same drinks you already had, or would you like to try something else?"

Craft looked at me briefly before focusing back on the waitress. "Yes, another double shot of Hennessy for me and another margarita for her."

"I'm sorry. What kind of margarita was it again please?"

"Mango margarita but with Hennessy."

"Okay, coming right up."

"Thank you."

"Okay, let's see if I will be returning with you." Craft took a bite of one of the wings before sampling everything.

Chapter 5

Craft

"Superstar!" My barber, Sean, shouted when I stepped inside the barbershop.

"Man, get out of here." I made my way over and dapped him up.

"Got me doing house calls and having tea parties." The shop erupted in laughter.

"Nah, you on your own with that part. Y'all should have seen this nigga sitting on the floor Indian style, sticking his pinky out." I clowned as I walked around the shop, dapping up the fellas.

"You know I love the kids, and it breaks my heart to tell them no."

"Soft ass." A barber named Greg clowned.

"Nigga, I remember when baby girl P had you changing the channel from a ball game to her favorite cartoon so ease up off me." Sean called him out, making the shop erupt in laughter once again.

There was never a dull moment when I came by the shop. Sean used to cut hair out of his mother's garage. He had been cutting my hair since I was in junior high and had no business letting him put clippers to my head. He used to always say he was never working in anybody's shop; then, three years ago, he made the announcement that he was moving to a shop. Sean was a few years older than me and used to run the streets with my cousin. He used to have the biggest crush on my sister all through high school, but my sister hardly paid him any mind. She was into older dudes with big pockets. When she hooked up with Peace's dad, Sean gave up his chase. I remember when she passed, Sean used to always say, "Man, if I never gave up chasing." But my sister was into what she was into, even if it meant her no good.

"I got two in front of you, and then, I got you."

"Alright."

"How are my baby girls doing?"

"You know Skylar is still bossy and full of energy; then Peace is chilling."

"So, check this out. I'm trying to come to one of your little single mixers." Greg announced.

"It's speed dating, and we have one this coming Friday. But I know you're going to need time to get yourself together, so I'll drop off flyers for the next one."

"Need time to get myself together? What are you trying to say?"

"Your pretty boy ass be needing the whole week to get ready for the club Saturday night."

"What? I take pride in how I look." Greg shrugged.

"I don't know any other grown man that picks his clothes out for the week." Sean cut his clippers off and spun his client's chair around as he finished his cut.

"It's called time management." Greg defended himself as the bell above the shop door rang as the door opened, and we all looked to see who was coming in.

Everyone quieted at the sight of Lovely's beautiful ass standing in the doorway.

"Hello, fellas." She greeted, stepping inside fully and closing the door.

"Hello." We all called out.

"You are so damn beautiful it's a crime." One dude I didn't know called out.

"Thank you." She acknowledged and made her way over to Sean.

"What up, boss lady?"

"Sean, I told you about that."

"Aye, Lovely, when you gone let me take you out? I've been asking you for the longest, and word around town you not with that preppy nigga no more." This nigga named Peewee called out.

"Peewee, the answer is and will always be no." She gave him a tight smile and focused back on Sean.

"You gone shoot me down like that?" He continued.

"Peewee, ease up." Sean warned.

Peewee threw up his hands in surrender.

"What's good, Lovely? What made you bless us with your heavenly presence today?"

"Yes, blessed by God himself." The nigga sitting beside me spoke.

That caused her head to shoot in our direction with her lip turned up. Her eyes surveyed the three of us that were sitting in this area, and when her eyes landed on me, her lips formed a smile as she took me in. I blew a kiss at her, and she quickly turned back and faced Sean.

"I called your phone and of course, like always, no answer."

"We prefer to see you anyway, all of you." The nigga beside me spoke again.

"Aye, my man, chill." I warned him.

"That's your girl or something?" he questioned.

"Nah, but..."

"Well, mind your business."

"Aye, my man, this is your first time here. So, you can either sit back, be quiet, and wait until it's your turn in a chair or you can bounce." Sean intervened.

The nigga sat back, not saying anything else.

"Maybe I should have continued calling until you picked up." Lovely started looking around the shop.

"You know we can be a little loud but no louder than y'all be down there. But I wasn't going to look at that phone until I finished cutting hair. You know that."

"Yes, busy man. Anyways, Halloween will be here before

we know it. I'm trying to see how many businesses I can get to participate in doing something for Halloween, whether you just decorate and pass out candy or if you can turn your shop into a mini haunted house. But not too scary though."

"That really sounds more like you tell me what I'm actually going to be doing."

"No, I'm asking, sir."

"Well, boss lady, you got it. Greg is going to dress up and pass out candy."

"Wait, what?" Greg stopped cutting his client's hair and turned to face them.

"You heard her, Greg. You have to dress up and pass out candy. Good thing is you have ample time to plan." Sean joked, and everyone laughed.

"Oh, no, sir. All the barbers need to participate. So, if you gentlemen will be dressed up and passing out candy, that would be much appreciated." She looked around.

"What?" They all questioned.

"It's for the kids, fellas." She shrugged her shoulders. "I'll have flyers by the second week of October. Thank you, fellas." She turned and made her way to the door. Stopping, she looked at me. "Hello, Mr. Carter."

"Hello, beautiful."

Smiling, she left the shop.

"Come on, man. Now I really don't stand a chance." Peewee fussed as soon as the door closed.

"Nigga, you got four kids and seven baby mommas. You never stood a chance." Sean clowned.

"Nigga like broads that bust his windows and owe Rent a Center." Another barber clowned, making everyone laugh as he and Sean clowned Peewee.

Lovely

After leaving the barbershop, I went across the street to my cousin's auto shop. Out of all the businesses on the block and in spite of him being my cousin, I knew his hermit behind would give me the hardest time. Walking in, I tapped the bell sitting on the receptionist desk because, like always, she wasn't at the desk.

"I'm coming." My cousin stepped inside with his face balled up as always.

"You are much too handsome to be always frowning."

"Girl, what you want, and where the fuck is Nina ass at? It's like I pay her to stay away from the front desk." He huffed, tossing the towel that he was using to wipe his hands on the desk.

"I don't see why you pay her at all." I shrugged my shoulders.

"Don't come over here trying to run my shit."

"I don't know how your business stays so busy with your rude ass." I grabbed the towel and threw it at him as he sat in the chair behind the counter.

"Niggas want they car to look better than the next nigga, and bitches bring they car through just to look at a handsome, mean ass nigga." He shrugged his shoulders. "Now, what do you want?"

Although mean as hell and as grumpy as an old man, my cousin was very handsome, so there was no doubt that women found any reason to bring their car here just to be close to him.

"I want to host a community event for Halloween."

"Okay, tell me how much you need and I got you." He prepared to stand from the chair.

"No, I was actually hoping you would turn your shop into a haunted house for the day." I rushed out.

"Nope, can't do it."

"Abiri." I whined.

"What are you in here begging for, girl?" My grandfather stepped inside.

"Hey, Papa."

"Hey, baby." He came over, leaned over the counter, and kissed my cheek.

"Papa, tell Abiri to let me turn his shop into a haunted house. I'm trying to do a Halloween event for the community."

"Abiri, let your cousin make this place into a haunted house."

"No can do."

"Nigga!" My papa kicked his leg. "You can turn the shop into a haunted house for my beautiful Reese's piece." My grandfather smiled at me.

"Old man, this my shit. You don't run anything around here."

"Fuck what you talking about." My grandfather raised his hand.

"I said no, and that's my final answer." Abiri stood from the chair.

"Nigga, are you bucking up at me?" My grandfather faced him, and they stood chest to chest.

"Man, I'm about to go back out there and finish working on that car. Ain't nobody fucking with you. But you better go ahead before I call Auntie Linda and have her make you sit your ass at home." Abiri shoulder bumped him as he passed by him to go back outside.

"I'ma fuck his big, grumpy ass up." My papa fussed.

I laughed at their antics. The two were always bickering. Ever since my grandfather let the gym go, his time was mostly spent at the shop with Abiri.

"Did you eat today?"

"You know I did. Your Aunt Linda cooked for that big ass boy out there last night. So, we had some hot water cornbread, baked salmon, rice, and broccoli."

"Hot water cornbread, Papa?"

"Yeah, Abiri just had to have some."

"Oh, well, I have to go talk to the rest of the businesses. I'm leaving work early today, so I can take you home when I'm ready if you like."

"No, thank you, baby. I'm going to hang with Abiri until he finishes."

"Alright, Papa." I kissed his cheek.

"I'll talk to him and see if I can get him to change his

mind."

"Thank you, Papa."

Chapter 6

Craft

After getting my hair cut, I picked up the girls from school. I took them for ice cream and then to my aunt's house before I headed to my gym, Match. Two nights out of the week, we hosted an after-hours fight club. It was an anything goes and come at your own risk club. Gloves and headgear if you desired. It was Honor's idea after a night out turned into a little brawl. I hosted training sessions for the youth Tuesdays and every other Saturday. Then, I got in the ring during after hours every other month.

"What's up, young one?"

"Mr. Nelson, the man, the myth, the legend, what's good?" I stood from my seat to give my mentor a hug.

"Are you getting ready to fight?"

"Yeah, a little something."

"Well, let me wrap your hands and we can do a little warm up."

I retook my seat while he grabbed the tape from the storage closet.

While he wrapped my left hand, the room was dead silent.

"What brings you by tonight?" I placed my right hand on the table, so he could wrap it.

"My Reese, as I like to call her, well, I heard that you took an interest in." He looked me square in my eyes, placing the tape down, pausing the wrapping of my right hand. "I love my kids, but my grands, especially my only two grand girls, I hold them close to my heart."

"Come on, Nelson."

"Nah, young one, let me finish. I know you, and I love you like you are one of my own, but my Lovely getting anything less than what she deserves will fuck up the love and respect I have for you. She already had one that wasted her time. I don't need you hanging around her if you're not going to treat her right."

"Come on, Nelson, what have you always told me?"

"Be better than me. I've done a lot of good, but with that good, I've done plenty of bad." We quoted together.

"You also told me your biggest regret was not treating your one right and not being the best father that you could be. You know I'm raising my daughter and niece. I'm not out here being reckless. I manage my businesses, and I take care of my girls. I'm trying to include Lovely."

Looking me in my eyes, he gave me a quick nod before wrapping my right hand. We did a few warmups before the knock on the door signaled it was time for me to fight.

"Aye, Nelson." I grabbed his shoulder, stopping him from walking out the door. "During the little time that I have had the opportunity to spend with Lovely, I know the inside is just as beautiful as the outside. She's giving me a hard time right now, but if she'll have me, I definitely won't fuck up."

"Alright, I'm going to hold you to that. I may be old, but I'll get in that ring with you." He pulled me in for a hug, patting my back extra hard like he always did when I was at the gym, training. He instilled a lot in me, gave me a lot of guidance. He made sure I went to community college and took business classes because he said that if this boxing shit didn't pan out, I needed a fallback plan. It definitely didn't pan out like I thought it would.

"Alright, young one, let me see if you still remember what I taught you."

I followed him to the ring. He stood by Honor while I stepped inside. The announcer went through his regular announcements. Then, me and my opponent were in the middle of the ring, touching gloves. The dinging of the bell took me into another space. Everything around me went quiet. When I was fighting, it was like everything outside those ropes went black, and I didn't see anything but my opponent, and till this day, I didn't hear anything but Nelson coaching me in my head. He used to tell me, "Before you step in the ring, shake everything off. Nothing matters but the man in front of you."

A bell and five rounds later, I walked out the ring with another win and was sore as hell.

"Alright, young one, you still got a little something going on." Nelson boasted.

"Don't lie to his ass. He was moving a little slow. Didn't think he was going to come out on top." Honor popped some Skittles in his mouth.

"Man, wrap up. I'll show you slow."

"Yeah, yeah." He waved me off.

Nelson stayed around to unwrap my hands and wrap ice packs around my hands and ribs.

I could admit tonight wasn't a joke.

Once all fights were finished, winners were paid, and the cleaning service had my gym clean and ready to open back up in the morning. Honor and I locked down and headed to our cars well after three in the morning.

"Aye, are you coming to the homecoming game tonight?"

"Of course. I can't miss that. Orion wouldn't let me live that down. This his senior year. You know I have to be there for everything."

"Yeah, he might try to get in the ring with you next."

"Yeah, alright!" We both laughed.

"Are you going home or to Mom's?"

"Going to Mom's would be safer but I'm trying to get some sleep."

"You know you're more than welcome to crash at my spot."

"With that bird you got that's always clucking, I'll pass. I still got beef with you for letting Aster get away, and you still putting up with that loudmouth bird." I shook my head at him.

"Yeah, I know, man. I definitely fucked up." He leaned against his car, running his hand down his face. "But if the man upstairs blesses me to be in her presence ever again, I swear I'll do whatever needs to be done to have her by my side again."

"Well, let's hope he blesses you because I'm real close to paying Wise to rock Amber shit. I don't even know why you still deal with her."

"Man, you know the story."

"Aye, that bullshit happened three years ago, and if you ask me, she was a part of it. Got you around here feeling guilty about some shit. You gotta shake that shit. But I'm out." I slid in my car, starting it. I waited for Honor to do the same. Once he pulled off, I made a U-turn and a quick left to get to the freeway.

Hopping on the 110 freeway, I rolled my windows down, so the cold air could hit my face, and turned my radio up, so I could stay awake on this drive home. By the time I hit the 405 freeway, my eyes were burning, and I couldn't stop yawning. Observing my surroundings, I pushed down on the gas, pushing eighty. Hitting my exit on Cherry, I made it to Burnett. Turning my radio down and rolling my windows up, I drove up the hill to my little community. Pulling in my driveway and cutting my car off, I rested my head on the headrest, shutting my eyes momentarily. Finally finding the energy, I got out of my car and sluggishly walked up my walkway and to my door. Stepping inside, although tired, it felt good to be home. Heading straight to my bedroom and into my bathroom, I turned the water on, stripped out of my clothes, and hopped in the shower. I took a quick, ten-minute shower and didn't bother drying off. I dove right in my bed. I planned to sleep as long as I could. My eyes were closed, and sleep took over as soon as my head hit the pillow.

Chapter 7

Glen

"Glen, it's October!" My mother stepped into Sasha's apartment where I had been staying since my grandfather gave us the timeframe to move out.

"Hello to you too, Mother." I closed and locked the door, walking past her and taking a seat back on the couch. She stood awkwardly by the door, clutching her purse. "Care to have a seat?"

"Absolutely not. I don't plan on standing… I mean, staying long."

"How can I help you today?"

"How can you help me? It's officially October, and every time I call you to discuss what you plan to do to get that girl back, you say you're working on it, but it looks to me like you don't care!" She snapped, waving her hand around.

"Look, I feel fucked up about what I helped you do, and at this point, I no longer want any parts."

Quickly walking over and standing in front of me, she bent down so that we were eye level.

"If you think that I'm going to allow you to fuck up what I worked so hard for, then you can end up in the ground too!" She spoke through clenched teeth, pointing her finger in my face. "All of a sudden, you want to grow a conscience. Well, it's too late."

"Momma…"

"Stop calling me that shit!" She yelled. "Glen, I need you to get dressed and go get that girl back instead of over here playing house. You sure know how to pick them."

"Gwen..." I started.

"I don't need you talking. I need you up and moving."

"Daddy, we're back." Sasha walked through the door with the baby. "Oh, hey. Glen didn't tell me you were coming by. Did you come to see the baby, maybe watch him for a couple of hours?" Sasha placed the car seat down and removed the baby, trying to hand him over to Gwen.

"Girl, please." Gwen pushed the baby back. "Get that baby away from me."

"Excuse you?" Sasha hugged the baby close and stepped back.

"Sasha, please just go to the back and allow me a moment to speak to my mother."

Rolling her eyes and smacking her lips, she stomped to the room, making sure to slam the door.

"Glen, I made sure you had a wonderful life. I left you in your grandparents' care when I could have just left you in that hospital to end up in anyone's care. You owe me, Glen!" She spoke through gritted teeth, standing over me.

"I owe you?" I stood from my seat.

"Yes, you owe me because I afforded you the life that you live!" She yelled.

Chuckling, I stepped away from her, angry. Angry with her, with myself. All my life, I sought her approval and craved her love when I should have been solely focusing on the two people that mattered the most, that poured into me, and loved me when the person that should have been doing all that could care less about me.

I opened the front door. "I need you to leave." Her face went from shock to anger.

Making her way over to me, she stopped in front of me. "The check is only good for one hundred eighty days. We've already wasted one hundred twenty. You better figure out a way for me to get this money or so help me God."

"You originally said the money was for us. But I'm glad I see the truth. Goodbye, Gwen!" I waited for her to step out, and I slammed the door in her face. Smacking the door, I rested my head against it.

"What was that about? What money, Glen?"

"Were you listening to my conversation?" I turned and looked at Sasha. "I thought I told you to go to the room?"

"This is my house, Glen, and I'm not a child." She rolled her eyes.

Moving past her, I slid my shoes on, grabbed my jacket and keys, and left. I fucked up my life for a woman that was selfish and self-centered, and sadly, I was so much like her.

Lovely

"Aye, turn that up!" Wise yelled with her hands in the air, winding her hips.

"All my friends, all my kin saying Wise just let that end. But I breathe you." She belted out.

Wise was beautiful and talented all around. She should be on someone's stage, but she said her hands belonged in someone's hair or blinging someone's nails out. With the confidence she exuded, she would be on someone's pole if you let her.

"Oh, this what we doing today? Today a Monica day? Who door I have to kick down?"

"Ask Gorgeous, she controlling the radio. You good, baby?" I nudged her as I parted her hair.

"Yes." She answered barely above a whisper.

"Why aren't you at school today? Isn't it homecoming?" Wise questioned as she went back to twisting her client's locs.

"Yes, but I'm not going."

"Why not?" I spun her chair around, so she could face me.

"I just don't want to." She mumbled with her head down.

"Gorgeous, what's going on, baby?" I gently grabbed her chin and lifted her head up.

"It's nothing. I just don't want to go."

I took a moment, trying to read her. Before I could question her further, her phone started ringing. The name Orion displayed on her screen.

"Who's Orion?"

"Nobody!" She pulled her face from my hand and looked down at her phone as she rejected the call.

"You know I love you, and you can talk to me about anything, right?"

"Yes, can I go to the bathroom please?" Her voice cracked.

"Yes." I stepped back and allowed her space to get up.

She hopped up from the chair and rushed to the bathroom while we all watched on.

"I'll tell you one thing. If somebody at that school fucking with her, you gone be bailing me out of jail!" Wise snapped as soon as the bathroom door closed.

The bell for the front door dinged, grabbing all of our attention, before anyone could respond to Wise.

"Here goes the wicked bitch of Ladera Heights!" Wise hissed while rolling her eyes at Glen's mother, Gwen.

"Little girl."

"Lady, I will beat your ass. You know better than to talk to me." Wise rolled her eyes.

"Low class."

"Low class? Honey, you're low class, just dressed up. If it wasn't for your parents, your old ass wouldn't have shit. Not a pot to piss in or window to throw it out of. I have my own home. I don't live in my parents' pool house!" Wise snapped, waving the comb in her hand. "Like I said, you know better than to talk to me. My friend is nice, not me. I'll go to jail for elder abuse for happily beating your ass!" She turned back to her client, leaving Gwen standing there with her mouth open and holding her chest.

"Gwen, how can I help you?" I pulled her from her state of shock.

She looked from me to Wise and back at me. "I came to talk to you about my son."

"There is nothing to talk about, so if that's all, have a good day."

"Excuse me?"

"Your son and I are no longer together, so there is nothing to discuss."

"I understand you two had a misunderstanding."

"Misunderstanding?" Wise snorted.

Gwen cut her eyes in her direction before focusing back on me.

"Gwen, him disrespecting me, cheating on me, and having a child during our relationship that isn't mine isn't a misunderstanding. Now if you didn't come to get your hair done..."

"Which you desperately need and not to mention those nails." Wise rolled her eyes.

"Then I will have to ask you to leave please."

"I tried to be nice to you, not so little girl."

"Yup, that'll do it." Wise grabbed her by the back of her shirt. "You don't have to go home, but you have to get the hell out of here!" Wise dragged her to the door with Kevin running in front of her and pushing the door open, allowing Wise to push Gwen out. "Don't come back." Wise pulled the door shut while we all watched Gwen gather herself and stomp off.

I was happy it was still early, and we only had three clients in the shop. I prided myself on my salon being a place of solace, but Glen had made it nothing but a shit show these past couple of weeks.

"I see myself beating her old ass when it's all said and done." Wise huffed on her way back to her station.

"I don't think you need to be at the first station anymore." I giggled.

"Nah, I need to be the first line of defense."

"Lord, Wise, what am I going to do with you?"

"Love me like you've been doing." She winked before focusing back on her client.

I headed to the back to check on my sister. My sister was

quiet but could have her outspoken moments, but the her she was showing me today was not her. I hadn't seen my sister sad in a while.

"Gorgeous, can I come in, sweetie?" I knocked on the bathroom door, just to announce my presence. "Gorgeous, I'm coming in," I announced after I stood there for a moment without a response from her. Stepping in, I entered the bathroom, passing the sitting area. I stopped in front of the closed stall door and listened to my sister cry. "Gorgeous, honey, what's wrong?"

"I'm stupid. I'm just so stupid." She cried.

"What happened? Gorgeous, come out please."

She cried harder.

"I can't help you if you don't talk to me."

"My momma left me; my father didn't want me. Then the one boy that I wanted to notice me, he only likes me as a friend and then..." She broke out into a sob.

"Gorgeous Blessed Reynolds, don't talk like that and open this door right now before I call Daddy!" I smacked my hand against the door.

A few minutes passed before the stall door opened, and I was looking into my sister's saddened face. I opened my arms as she fell into my chest and cried hard. Wrapping my arms around her, I held her tightly and allowed her to cry. Once her sobs turned into whimpers, I pulled back, cupping her chin and lifting her face.

"Momma didn't leave you by choice. Forget the man whose sperm created you. You are beautiful, and the guy that's for you will come when he's ready to be the man you need." Pulling her over to the sink, I grabbed a few Kleenexes to clean her face. "You are not stupid. Don't ever let me hear you say that again." I looked her in the eyes as I wiped her face. "You know you can talk to me about anything, right?"

She nodded her head before wrapping her arms around me and dropping her head on my chest.

"You are loved, Gorgeous, and whatever is weighing on

you, release it. I'm here whenever you are ready."

"Okay." She murmured in my chest.

"So, do you want me to take you home?"

She released me and stepped back. "No, I can finish getting my hair done."

"Are you sure? I don't have any appointments today. Once I'm done with you, we can go to lunch and do whatever you would like for the rest of the day."

The bathroom door opening grabbed both of our attention.

"Is everything alright?" Wise stepped inside, allowing the door to close behind her.

"Yes, I'm okay." Gorgeous stepped back to the sink and grabbed more Kleenex to dry her face again.

"What's wrong, Gorgeous?" Wise questioned, walking over and standing behind her, rubbing her back.

"Nothing." Gorgeous answered while shifting her eyes to the floor.

Wise looked at me momentarily before focusing back on Gorgeous .

"Hey, look at me." She spun her around, placing a finger under her chin and tilting her head up. "What is going on with you, Gorgeous, and you know we can sit in here all night until you are ready to tell me?" Wise sternly stated, placing her hands on her hips.

Gorgeous leaned against the bathroom sink and sighed. "I've just been a little sad about my mother not being here and having the chance to experience her like Lovely did. And I know Jasper loves me as if he is the man that assisted in my existence because he named me after him and has loved me from the beginning. But it still hurts at times that the man that's part of the reason that I am here can care less about me. I mean, you see the checks that he was sending recently stopped coming."

"First and foremost, don't let Daddy hear you call him Jasper. You are his daughter, and he doesn't love you any less. In his mind, he and Momma laid down and created you. Do I wish things could be different and Momma could still be here? Yes. Hell, I wish our grandmother could be here as well, but you know they're watching over us."

"I know." She wiped the tears that rolled down her face.

"So, is that all that's bothering you?" Wise questioned.

"Just some high school stuff but I will be fine." She shrugged.

"Is someone at school bothering you?"

"Yes, but it's nothing I can't handle."

"If someone is bothering you, we need to know because you know I can't stand no bullying mess." I looked over at Wise and saw her right eye twitching a bit, signaling that she was getting riled up.

"Just this girl and her friends trying to pick at me about a boy."

"Do you like this boy?" Wise leaned against the bathroom sink with her.

"Yes, and just when I started feeling like he may like me back, I saw him kissing the same girl that doesn't like me because of him."

"Is that why you didn't go to school today?" I questioned.

"Sort of, and I just really didn't want to be bothered today."

"Oh, no, little baby, we are not going to start running from our problems at this early age."

"Right, so you're going to clean your face and come out front, so I can get you ready for the homecoming game." I hugged her.

"Yes, and Lovely and I will be going with you."

"Thank you."

"You're our little baby. We are going to always stand beside you and step behind you, beautiful." Wise assured her.

We headed out of the restroom to allow her some space to get herself together.

"I wonder what brought all that on. You know, your mom and her sperm donor." Wise whispered as soon as we stepped out of the bathroom.

"I'm not fully sure. Maybe we can take her out Sunday or something to talk to her more, especially about this little boy situation."

"Aww, our little baby having boy troubles?" Wise gushed.

"Wise, she don't need no boy troubles." I sighed.

"Lovely, she is seventeen and will be graduating next June. She is not five. Suck it up."

"I know, but she is still my sweet, innocent baby."

"How we know she innocent when she leave the house?" Wise squinted her eyes.

"Wise, don't start."

"What? I'm just saying. She didn't even tell us she had a crush. Don't you find that suspicious?"

"Wise, gone."

"Alright, fine." She raised her hands in surrender.

"Thank you."

"Seriously, though, there is nothing we can do about that man not being in her life, but as far as being sad about your mother, we can all climb in the bed together; watch movies, and drink soda and eat junk till we can't no more like we used to."

"You always coming through for us." I hugged her.

"I always will, and that little boy better hope she don't point him out tonight. I may have to fuck him up off GP."

Pulling away from her, I could only shake my head.

"What you shaking your head for? You already know how I'm coming."

"You need to leave peoples' kids alone." I made my way back to my station.

"No, people kids need to leave me alone."

"I've been saying for years that you fit the criteria to receive a monthly check."

"Whatever!" She smacked her lips, heading to her station.

I sat in my styling chair, waiting for Gorgeous to return from the bathroom. I hoped our little talk was enough to pull her from her funk.

Chapter 8

Lovely

"It's a little chilly. I knew I should have brought a sweater." I wrapped my arms around myself as we walked through the parking lot, heading to the football field.

"Girl, you have on jeans, a sweater top, and boots. You will be just fine during this game." Wise walked ahead of me in some jeans, a quarter sleeve top, and some sandals because, as she claimed, her and closed toe shoes didn't get along.

I slipped my arm into Gorgeous' arm and pulled her closer to me. "Warm me up, little baby." I called her by the nickname Abiri had called her since bringing her home.

"You're so dramatic!" She laughed.

Once she came out of the bathroom after our little talk, she seemed lighter. The sadness still lingered, but she laughed at Wise's antics like everyone, especially when the booster came by for his weekly visits, and he and Wise argued about his prices until she threatened to call the police on him as she always did. Then, he gave her a deal to buy everything he had on hand, which she did, and after talking all the mess she did, she still gave him more than what he asked for. But that was Wise, the light in everyone's life that she came in contact with.

"Girl, it is cold."

"Well, if you popped your pills like you're supposed to, maybe you wouldn't be so cold all the time."

I stopped in my tracks and reared my head back. “Little girl, I just know you didn’t just snap on me like that?”

“What? I’m just saying.” She shrugged her shoulders and pulled me along while Wise laughed as we stepped in line to get our tickets to enter the game.

“If you didn’t ditch school today, you could have gotten our tickets.” Wise fussed while looking around.

“Hush, impatient one. There is only three people in front of us.”

“You know them girls by the gate, little baby?” Wise tapped Gorgeous on her shoulder, causing her and I to look in the direction that Wise was pointing. We focused on a group of three girls leaning on the gate.

“Yes.” Gorgeous rolled her eyes.

“Is there an issue?”

“Yes, they have an issue with me, but I can care less about them.”

“Well, what is the issue, and you should have let me know beforehand. I would have laced my sneakers up for you today.”

“I’m not worried about them. Like you two always say, ‘As long as no one puts their hands on me, then there is no real issue.’”

“That’s right, little baby. But today, if they keep staring, they gone have to call they mommas cause I’ma have to touch somebody.” Wise threatened while looking directly at them and raising her voice so that they knew she was speaking about them.

“Next in line.” The ticket attendant called out, grabbing our attention.

“One student and two adult tickets please.” Gorgeous stepped up to the window.

“Well, hello, Gorgeous, my angel. I love how you always keep that hair of yours looking nice.”

“Thank you, Ms. Lamar. It’s all thanks to my sister.” Gorgeous looked back at me briefly, causing the lady in the ticket booth to lean over and look at me.

She smiled at me momentarily before focusing back on Gorgeous.

"I missed you in the library today, and you know I would have given you a few tickets for the game."

"I needed a break today, but I'll be seeing you Monday."

"Alright, baby, and ignore them heffas. You are beautiful effortlessly, and we all have our shortcomings and battles we must fight. Hold your head up and pay them no mind." She handed her the tickets and change.

"Thank you, Ms. Lamar." Gorgeous looked at us briefly before heading to the gate to enter the game.

"Pig." One of the girls called herself mumbling, causing them all to laugh.

"Being funny will get a little bitch and her friends beat up." Wise sang, halting their laughter.

They all stared but didn't open their mouths to make another sound as we walked through the gate.

"Are they the reason you didn't go to school today?" I leaned into Gorgeous and questioned in a low tone.

"Can we just enjoy the game?" She rolled her eyes.

"We are going to enjoy this game, but you are definitely going to tell us something."

"Those are just some dumb girls that don't like me because of a boy. But I don't get why. He doesn't like me like that."

"Who is the boy? Can we go to the concession stand first?" Wise stood on the other side of Gorgeous.

"One of the star players on the football team. Although he is very handsome and I've had a crush on him since tenth grade, it was a crush from a distance. I didn't even start talking to him until last year when we got paired together in English class. That's when a lot of girls started having an issue with me."

"Wait, how come I don't know about this boy?" I questioned as we maneuvered around the crowd heading to the concession stand.

"You actually met him. I did a biology project with him last year as well. Remember you had to leave the shop to bring some supplies to my classmate's house? Then you picked me up later that night?"

"Oh, the cutie that I said it was no way he was in high school?" I thought back to the final grade assignment that nearly stressed her out.

"Yes, him."

"Well, damn, the secrets I see."

"It's not like that." Gorgeous rolled her eyes while stepping in line.

"Well, what's it like?"

"You just weren't with her when she came. Your bad." Gorgeous patted Wise's back while Wise shook her hand off.

"Let me find out you salty." Gorgeous pinched her cheek.

I loved our moments like this.

"Can I get nachos with just cheese and a chili cheese hot link?"

"Make that two." Wise and I spoke at the same time.

Gorgeous glanced at us. "Okay, three chili cheese hot links, a pack of sour Skittles, and a blue Gatorade, the cool blue one." Gorgeous ordered.

"Okay, will that be all?"

"No, please can you add a Pepsi, can I get a slush mixed, hot Cheetos, and you may as well make it three orders of nachos with just cheese." Wise added to the order for the both of us.

"Okay, will that be all?"

Gorgeous looked at us to make sure. "Yes, that will be all."

The young girl behind the counter recited our order and the total before taking payment and giving us our change along with a ticket for our order.

"I can't remember the last time I went to a football game." We stepped to the side to wait for our order.

"Oh, Lovely, please. You barely wanted to do anything in high school. I had to drag you to our ten-year reunion."

"You did not have to drag me."

"Beg and drag, yes, I did. You were still laying around in your robe when I got to your house. Good thing I came as early as I did and with my hair products at that. If I hadn't secretly ordered the dress, you definitely wouldn't have gone."

"Whatever."

"So, what number is this little boy on the team?" Wise focused her attention on Gorgeous.

"Wise." Gorgeous groaned.

"Wise nothing. I have to see if the little boy is worth me catching a charge for you."

"Order 33."

"Good, the food is ready." Gorgeous rushed up to the window with us following behind her.

We each grabbed our items, and Wise and I followed behind Gorgeous to find some seats.

"Aye, Skylar, you can't just be running off like that." A deep voice yelled out as a little girl collided with my legs, causing me to drop my nachos and link to grab ahold of her, making sure she didn't fall back.

"Hey, don't run from your father. You can get lost in the crowd." I looked down at her, getting a good look, and realizing it was Skylar.

"Sorry about that." I looked up at Honor.

"Hey."

"Hey, what are you doing here?" He gave me a quick hug.

"My little sister attends this school." I pointed over at her and Wise.

"Hello." He spoke to Gorgeous. "What up, wild Wise?" He hugged her.

"Hey yourself."

But I held on to her because he definitely wasn't Craft.

"Hey, I remember you."

"You," he looked down at Skylar, "you know better than to be running off."

"I was just coming to say hi, cousin Honor. She did my hair. I just wanted to say hi." She smiled brightly at him.

"Yes, but you still don't just take off. You tell me what you're trying to do, and I will help you do it." He chastised her.

"Now you're going to have your auntie fussing at me, and you made Ms. Lovely drop her food."

"I'm sorry." She dropped her head.

"Pick your head up, just remember to communicate. If your dad was here, you would not have just ran off." He picked her up and put her on his shoulders. "Please allow us to get you some more." He dug in his pocket and pulled out a couple of bills. He handed me twenty and put the rest back.

"That will be the honorable thing to do." Wise snarked.

"Here you go."

"I want some food too, cousin Honor."

"Okay, we have to find your auntie and P, and I'll get my favorite ladies something to snack on. You ladies have a nice day, and Wise, don't make me make a phone call."

Wise glanced at me and smacked her lips. "I'm not worried about what you're talking about."

He quickly looked between the two of us. "I bet, but you ladies enjoy the game." He turned and made his way through the crowd.

"Okay, so back to the concession stand we go." Gorgeous turned, heading back while the two of us followed her.

Craft

I answered my phone as I exited the highway.

"I'm not too far out."

"Your lady up here."

"What?" I turned my music down to hear him better.

"I said your lady is here."

"Oh, yeah, who is she with?"

"Wise crazy ass and then you know the young girl that Orion was asking us advice about. His classmate that he seemingly always get paired with for assignments."

"Don't be talking about my baby." I heard my aunt in the background.

"Whatever. Aye, hurry up so you can feed these kids."

"Honor, get your tail up and go get my babies some

snacks." My aunt fussed.

"You better go feed her babies before she whoop you in front of everybody at the game." I laughed, thinking about no matter how old we were, my aunt had no problem showing us who was boss.

"You funny. That's why your girl sitting next to this buff nigga right now, grinning." He laughed.

"That's why yours left you." I laughed after he abruptly hung the phone up in my face.

I turned my music back up and continued the short distance to the school. Tonight was my little cousin's homecoming game. He was a beast on the field, and I was not just saying that because he was my little cousin. College coaches had been reaching out since he was in tenth grade. Over the summer, we took a few college tours, and he put in many applications. He was leaning toward USC if he stayed home, Jackson State University or Baylor if he went away. My little cousin was very talented, and I was proud of him. Not only was he good on the field, but when it came to academics, many were blown away with how smart he was. My aunt never played when it came to that schoolwork. Education over recreation was what she always preached. If Orion's grades weren't up to par, she would definitely pull him from the field. But if football didn't get him into college, his grades definitely would.

Pulling into the school, I cruised around, looking for a spot. When I didn't find one, I exited the lot and cruised down the street until I found a spot about a block away. Securing my car, I hustled back to the school because the game was scheduled to start soon. Making it through the parking lot, I stopped at the ticket booth to get my entry ticket before heading inside. Walking down the walkway, I looked between the bleachers and in front of me, looking for my family and watching my steps.

"Daddy!" A voice that I would never get tired of shouted out.

I looked up, and Skylar was standing on the bleachers, waving her hands, while Honor held on to her legs. I smiled at her before making my way up the bleachers.

"Daddy!" Skylar yelled excitedly, trying to leap over Honor once I made it to where they were sitting. But luckily, Honor had a hold of her because she would have been landing on the ground.

"Aye, chill, girl. You're already on your strike one for running off." My aunt fussed, grabbing her and making her sit down. "You know better than that. Just because your dad is here doesn't mean act up. You wait until he gets to you."

Skylar looked at my aunt, nodding her head, then snapped her head in my direction, giving me a big smile. I slid in, picking Skylar up and sitting her on my lap once I sat down.

"Hey, my love." I kissed the top of Skylar's head. "Hey, P." I kissed Peace on the temple.

"Hey." She quickly acknowledged me before going back to eating her nachos.

"Why are you acting up, about to have your aunt mad up here?" I tickled Skylar.

"I wasn't acting up!" She giggled.

"Oh, so what's this I hear about you running off?" I stopped tickling her.

"I just wanted to say hi to my friend."

I lowered her to the bleacher, allowing her to stand up, and turned her around so that she was now facing me.

"Hey, you know better than running off. You could have gotten lost. Then what would you have done?"

"I just wanted to see my friend." Her eyes watered.

I pulled her to me and hugged her briefly. Pulling back, I looked at her.

"I already talked to her about it, and she's not going to do it anymore. Right, little cuz?" Honor reached out with his fist balled up.

"Right." Skylar balled her fist, and they bumped fists.

"So, who is this friend you just had to see?"

"Ms. Lovely!" She beamed.

"Oh, yeah, that's your friend?"

"Yes, Daddy, and I want to go back to her, so she can do my hair pretty again."

"I'll see what I can do, but these braids still look nice." I tugged one of her braids.

"Behind you, four rows up." Honor whispered in my ear.

Looking behind me, I didn't even try to be discreet. Lovely sat there, laughing at something Wise was saying. I watched them interact for a few more moments before turning back around as the band and cheerleaders made their entrance. Everyone stood and cheered as the players made their way on the field. As the yelling of players' names and clapping settled, everyone took their seats.

"Tonight, we are going to do things differently." The coach spoke into the microphone while standing on the bench. "With it being the homecoming game, we would like to acknowledge the senior players. As well as they will be giving a rose to someone that is special to them, may it be a parent, teacher that has helped them along the way, or so on. But as we're finishing the season, I want to thank my team, their support system, the faculty, and students that come out to every game. So, I'm going to call the names in order starting with Daniel Adams."

The player went to the coach and hugged him as he told him something before handing him a rose. He called five more players, and we watched as Orion was next. He had been standing in line, looking around anxiously. He smiled and nodded in our direction.

"Now this young man, I am truly proud of. We have had a few bumps in the road, but he has never hit a dead end. Orion Carter." The stands erupted in whistles, applause, cheers, girls yelling his name, and a few other things. I watched the coach repeat the same actions. Orion grabbed the rose and jogged off the field, heading to the bleachers. He jogged down the walkway and jogged up the stairs leading to where we were seated. Honor and I stood as he headed our way, but when he got to us, he passed us. Honor and I quickly looked back to see where he was headed. He jogged up to the row Lovely was on, and he slid past them to a young girl that favored Lovely. Bending down, he handed her the rose and kissed her forehead. He then leaned and whispered something in her ear. It was like everyone went silent. Once he headed back down the bleachers, one girl that was a couple of rows in front of us stepped in his pathway.

"Really, Orion, you give her the rose? That fat slut."

"I thought I told them little heffas to watch they mouth when it come to you?"

I looked back, and Lovely was holding Wise's arm as she tried to get up while the young lady sitting beside Lovely looked embarrassed and as if she wanted to cry.

When I looked back in Orion's direction, he was already jogging down the pathway, heading back to the field.

I watched my little cousin until he fully made it back on the field. I looked back at Lovely. She was now on the phone with her face scrunched up.

"Momma, how your son just curve you like that?"

I looked in my cousin's direction then at my auntie, who just rolled her eyes.

"He just walked right past you, and you just sat here and let him." Honor continued.

"Boy, I really wish you would stop talking to me. I am tired of you." My aunt reached behind me and attempted to pop my cousin.

"Girl, please."

"I got your girl. Keep it up, Honor. You have been working every nerve that I have all day. I don't understand it. You have a whole condo but stay invading my space. I can't even cuddle with my man because you be moping around our house."

"Momma, please cut the theatrics because you damn sure don't be complaining when I be running all your errands."

"Cuss at me again and watch me embarrass you at this game."

"Momma, I'm a grown man."

"A grown man that's scared to stay at his house."

"I'm not scared. I just don't want to be there at the

moment."

"No, you don't want to be around your dependent is more like it. I don't know why you just don't put that girl out and be done with her. Made my best girl leave me." She smacked her lips.

"Whatever, Ma."

"Yeah, it's always whatever when you don't want to hear the truth."

"Auntie, where Unc at?" I questioned to get the attention off of Honor.

"He's home, laying down."

"His old ass was complaining that his back hurt." Honor laughed.

"Well, if you had helped him move the shelf in the garage like I told you to then his back wouldn't be hurting." My auntie balled up her napkin and threw it at him as the announcer announced the game was about to start.

We all focused on the field. The game was intense and a close game until the fourth quarter. My cousin and two other players turned it up a notch and took control on the field, allowing them to win the game by three field goals. In true football fashion, they dumped the water cooler on the coach. As everyone started filing out, we stayed seated to let the traffic ease up. My aunt wanted to wait for Orion, who I was sure wanted to probably hang out with his teammates.

"Honor, tell your little brother don't make me have to see him about my little baby. Got these little heffas fucking with her behind him." We both looked over as Wise slid on the bench beside him.

"Somebody momma gone get enough of you one day, always fucking with somebody kid." Honor shook his head.

"Hi, Gorgeous, honey, how are you? I haven't seen you in a while." I looked at my aunt and then followed her line of sight. I looked at Lovely and the young girl that was standing beside her on the stairs.

"Hi, Mrs. Carter. I've been doing well." She spoke with her head down slightly.

"Now what did I tell you about that? Hold your head up. You're too beautiful to be looking down at the ground."

She lifted her head at my aunt's words.

"That's more like it. Believe me, it is a reason you caused an uproar tonight." My aunt chuckled, and that caused her to slightly laugh as well. "Now, who are these two beautiful women with you?"

"This is my older sister, Lovely, and my sister from another, Wise." She introduced them to my aunt.

"Hello, ladies. I am Orion's mother."

"Hello." They both spoke in unison.

"Hi, Lovely." I smiled up at her.

"Hello, Craft." She smiled slightly.

"I'm glad you dropped that Mr. Carter."

"Well, if I recall, I didn't have a choice."

"Oh, you had a choice. You're just choosing to take the long route." I winked at her.

"May I ask how the two of you know each other, seeing as to how smitten my nephew is with you?"

"That's my friend, Lovely. That's who did these braids with the beads when that boy cut my ponytail." Skylar bounced up from her seat, making her way over to Lovely.

"Miss Busybody, I was talking to your dad."

"It's cool, Auntie, but yes, that's our friend, Lovely." I spoke, not taking my eyes off her.

"Your friend too, huh?" I looked in the direction of my aunt, who had a sleeping Peace, who had her headphones on to drown out all the noise tonight, tucked under her left arm, unlike an always energetic Skylar.

"Yes, my friend." I winked at my aunt.

"This must be the friend that Honor was telling me about."

"You complain about him always being at your house, but the two of you love gossiping with each other."

"I don't gossip. I just share things with my mother." Everyone burst out in a laugh.

"What's gossip, Daddy?"

"Nothing, child." My aunt quickly answered. "Lovely, I do appreciate you getting my babies' hair together because Lord knows the fast girls my nephew was letting do their hair just was not it."

"Well, I did precious Skylar's hair, and my best friend here, Wise, did the little beauty that is over there sleeping." She giggled. "But thank you. It was my pleasure."

"Well, I appreciate the two of you, and you did some good work. I didn't have to take them right back down this time. I don't know if whoever he was taking them to was trying to make them bald, but they would have my babies' heads braided up so tight."

"Oh, no, we can't have that. They're in good hands now." Wise interjected.

"Momma!"

Hearing my cousin's voice caused us all to look in his direction. He jogged toward us with a big smile. Jogging up the bleachers, he stopped at Lovely's sister.

"Hey, best friend." He hugged her.

"Orion, no, you're still sweaty." She tried to push him off.

"As my best friend, you're suppose to accept all of me."

"I told you about that best friend stuff, and my best friend, Joy, has told you I don't have room for another best friend."

"I'm not worried about the little noise you and Joy be making. I was calling you all day today. Why weren't you at school today?"

I sat back, watching my cousin and how he interacted with the young lady that I now knew was named Gorgeous.

"Look at my little brother, having a little crush." Honor just had to call him out.

Everyone turned their attention on Honor.

"Honor, come on over here and grab Peace, will you, and leave your brother alone."

"I didn't even do nothing to his little love-struck ass yet." Honor stood, stepping down to the next bleacher and walking over to my aunt and picking up Peace.

"Alright, I keep telling you about messing with my baby." My aunt popped him in the back of the head.

He flinched. "Everyone is your baby so which one?"

"You keep being funny, one of these days you gone pop up to my house, and the locks will be changed."

"Momma, you say that every other day. Be honest with yourself. You love having me over."

"Child, please. I can't wait till you have kids, so I can make sure they work your nerves like you do mine." She stood.

"Yeah, yeah, yeah. You just better come on before you get stuck riding with Orion."

"What's wrong with how I drive?" Orion stood with his arm draped over Gorgeous.

"Nothing at all, baby. Are the girls going home with me tonight?" My auntie questioned while picking up their trash.

"No, I got them tonight, but we'll be over tomorrow to see Orion off to his final homecoming dance."

"Gorgeous, are you going to the homecoming dance tomorrow night?"

"Yes, ma'am, I am."

"I've been trying to get her to ride with me, but she keeps turning me down."

"Lord, how could you deprive them of their common sense?" My aunt looked to the sky.

"What's that supposed to mean?" Both Honor and Orion asked.

"Nothing at all. Gorgeous, why don't you stop by before you head to the dance, so I can see how pretty you look, because I know you will be a showstopper tomorrow night?"

"Oh, she definitely will be beautiful as ever." Wise beamed.

"Yes, ma'am, I can do that."

"Okay, well, I'll be waiting on you. If you all are ready, I'm ready because this girl is tired."

"Yes, we can go. Come on, Sky." I stood and reached for Skylar's hand, who hadn't left Lovely's side.

"We can all walk together; I friend gets to her car safely." Orion

"You do not have to walk me.

"I hear you talking, but I'm st

"Whatever. Come on." She re her shoulder and headed down the l

"The two of them are so obliv watched the two of them.

"Yes, they both like each oth anything." Wise voiced.

"Yes, like someone else I know." Lovely mumbled but not low enough to where we couldn't hear.

We all followed suit, heading down the bleachers, with Skylar still stuck to Lovely, and it was a lovely sight that I could get used to.

"She's beautiful, nephew, and I see you're not the only one that likes her." My aunt grabbed ahold of my arm and whispered to me.

"She is beautiful." I glanced down at my aunt.

I could never express to this woman how much I loved and appreciated her. From the moment that she opened her door that night for my sister and I, and still till this day, she had been a rock for me with my sister's untimely passing and my daughter's mother feeling like a child wasn't what she wanted.

After getting pregnant, I told her the decision was totally up to her even though I knew I wasn't ready to be a father. But since I put myself in that situation, I was going to face the consequences. My aunt showed me the love my mother failed to while here on Earth. My father seemed to be her main priority. When my mother was alive, I always found solace at my aunt's home. Now being a single father and also having full guardianship over my niece, there were times my aunt would cook for both her home and mine. Even though I had a weekly cleaning service, she still came over and checked over the girls' rooms. She often shopped for both of our homes, kept the girls whenever I needed her to, and even when I didn't, her and my and asking for them. She did so much for all of ver complained or turned us away when we came

ye, Mrs. Lovely. I'll see you again, okay?" Skylar broke me ny thoughts.

I looked around, and we were standing close to Wise's truck.

"Bye, beautiful." Lovely bent down. and they hugged. "Good night, everyone." She called out, opening the passenger door.

"Good night, ladies. I look forward to seeing you tomorrow." My aunt waved.

"Yes, ma'am. We will be seeing you." She climbed in the truck as Wise started the car and rolled the windows down.

"You, little boy." She called out, pointing at Orion. "You played good tonight, but I hit harder than them boys on the field. Keep that in mind when it comes to this one." She pointed at Gorgeous, who sunk down in her seat and covered her face.

"I don't want any problems. That's my best friend for life."

"Yeah, well, you better check these heffas, or I'm going to check you." She threatened before pulling off.

"I like her." My aunt laughed.

"Ma, she just threatened me."

"I've been telling you to tell that girl how you feel. But no, you want to keep this best friend charade up. Keep it up and that's really all she's going to be. Now come on. It is cold." She headed over to Honor's car.

"Honor, I'm going to hop in the car with you. Swing me around to my car."

"For sure." He unlocked his car and put Peace in the backseat.

"Orion, are you coming straight home?" My aunt questioned, opening the car door.

"Yeah, you see how quick I came out the locker room. Wasn't trying to hang out tonight."

"You was just rushing to try to see your best friend. You

not fooling nobody." She got in the car.

He laughed and jogged over to his car. We waited for him to start it up, and once he pulled behind us, Honor pulled off.

Chapter 9

Lovely

"Look at you, little baby. You look damn good." Wise gushed as Gorgeous made her way down the stairs. The dress Wise picked out for her definitely fit her well and complimented her figure. It was a fitted, one strap dress that kind of bunched up around the stomach. They were having a masquerade ball theme. I pinned her hair to the side and curled it.

"So, I take it I look cute?" She spun around once reaching the bottom of the steps.

"You are just what your name is."

"You are beautiful, little baby." Abiri stepped up, kissing her forehead and handing her her mask.

"Thank you, favorite cousin." She hugged him.

"I think I need to chaperone cause I don't need these little niggas trying to get too close to you."

"Boy, bye." Wise pushed him back and stepped in front of Gorgeous.

"I know a corsage is for prom, but I'm extra so here." She grabbed Gorgeous' left wrist and slid it on. "I really love this dress on you."

"My little baby, and to think you been passing up homecoming all this time. Just wait until prom." I stepped up, lifting both her arms, taking her in.

"Why are you crying? You're going to make me cry. Stop it,

Lovely." She dabbed my eyes with her thumbs.

"You are just so beautiful."

"I hope we're not late." I looked behind me and watched my father and grandfather walk through my door.

"Look at my little one." My father walked in our direction with a bouquet of burgundy roses that matched Gorgeous' dress. "Hey, boss lady." My father hugged me and kissed my cheek before handing the roses to Gorgeous. "I'm not ready for this. I'm not ready for you to grow up too." He wrapped Gorgeous in his arms and held on to her.

"Let her go and let me give my doll baby some love." Our grandfather pushed him.

Pulling back, my father looked at her for a moment before releasing her and stepping to the side.

"Look at you. You're so beautiful, and you look just like your mother." My grandfather spoke, causing tears to well up in her eyes. "No, no, don't cry. You are far too beautiful to cry tonight." My grandfather pulled a handkerchief from his pocket and gently wiped her eyes.

"Well, we need to get going. She has to go by her friend's house."

"What friend?" All three men asked, looking at me.

"Oh, just Honor little brother." Wise's oh messy ass answered, grabbing her purse.

"Honor who?" Abiri's eyebrow hiked.

"Your friend, Honor."

"Oh, his little brother that be hanging around the auto shop sometimes? Oh, well, I guess we are all going."

"Oh, my God." Gorgeous groaned.

"Hush up, girl, and come on. He need to know who you have coming behind you." My grandfather followed Abiri out of the house.

"Is this guy your date?" My father questioned as I handed Gorgeous her purse.

"No, Pops, he's just my friend."

"Does he know that?"

"Yes, he knows. He's just my friend really, Pops."

"Alright. You will tell me if that changes, right?" My father held out his arm.

"Yes, Pops." Gorgeous smiled brightly while grabbing a hold of his arm.

I grabbed my purse and keys, following them out.

"You really do look beautiful tonight, doll baby." My father told her, helping her into the car.

"Thank you, Pops." She squeezed his hand before letting it go.

"Okay, I'm going to follow you all." He closed the door and hustled over to his car.

"Okay, you're going to have to guide me because I don't remember where I'm going."

"They live by King Hospital. Once you get over there, I will direct you." I pulled off with everyone following me.

We vibed to Monica, singing along on the way to Orion's house. Getting off the Wilmington exit as she instructed, I made a right when I got to 120th, passing the hospital. When we got to Central and 120th, I made a left.

"Okay, at the first street right here, make a right and go up that street. The house is going to be the fifth house. Well, the house with the truck parked on the grass right up there." Gorgeous pointed.

I pulled up and stopped in front of the house with Abiri behind me and my father behind him.

"Parking over here sucks. Hold on, let me call Orion and see if his mother can come out." She pulled her phone from her purse as the front door to the house opened.

"You all can just double park because there is really no parking, hence this child parked on my grass." Orion's mother yelled, coming down the steps and making her way over to the car.

I put the car in park, putting on my hazards. I turned my car off and got out to help Gorgeous out of the car.

"Look at you, girl." Orion's mother exclaimed, opening the door.

"Hi, Mrs. Marie."

"Excuse me, ladies. Let me help my little one out of the car." Abiri squeezed between us, assisting Gorgeous out of the car.

"Girl, you are so beautiful. Oh, yeah, they are going to be hating tonight." Mrs. Marie gushed. "And hello, Abiri. It has been a while since I have seen you. Why is that, Mister.?" She questioned Abiri as she hugged him.

"I've been working hard over at the shop, and I've taken an interest in someone, so she's been taking up my time."

"And she has replaced me in the kitchen too I see." She scrunched her brow while patting his stomach. "But that's a good thing. Treat her good, son."

"Oh, I see what's going on here." We looked at my father, and I followed his line of sight.

Standing on the porch, Orion, dressed in burgundy slacks with a cream-colored shirt, stood beside his brother, who was holding a plate of food.

"I thought you said he's just your friend, Gorgeous." My father stood beside me.

"We are, Pops." She rolled her eyes.

"Then why are the two of you dressed alike, like this a date?"

"Daddy, leave them alone. It's a school dance." I popped him on his chest.

"He don't even look like he in high school." My father grumbled.

"My baby is only seventeen." Orion's mother defended him.

"Orion, boy, you taking my grandbaby to the dance?"

My grandfather made his way over to the house.

"Pops, you know this little nigga?"

"Yeah, he brought his car to the shop, and I helped him work on it."

"More like you sat there and gave us instructions." Abiri mumbled.

My grandfather looked back at him, grilling him before continuing to make his way over to Orion.

"I want to see the princess. Orion said a princess was coming." Skylar burst out the house, dragging her cousin with her.

"Hey, slow down, girl." Mrs. Marie yelled as Skylar pushed past Orion and his brother, almost knocking my grandfather down.

"Oh, she is pretty like a princess!" Skylar yelled excitedly, stopping midway.

"She is pretty, isn't she?" Mrs. Marie pulled Gorgeous along with her, making her way toward the house.

"Your dress is so pretty!"

"Maybe we can get you one." I looked up at Craft, who now stood by his cousins, who were still planted on the porch.

"It's so pretty, Daddy!"

"Hi, Ms. Skylar and Ms. Peace. How are you two beauties?"

"Hi, Ms. Lovely. We are fine." Skylar spoke for the two of them, hugging my legs.

"Hey, little Ms. Peace." Wise scooped her up, and she gave Wise the biggest smile before hugging her.

"Come on, everyone. Let's go inside. I have food and drinks."

"Ma, we can't be getting all comfortable. We have to head out in a few." Orion groaned.

"Hush, boy. Y'all come on in here, so I can get some pictures."

Gorgeous just smiled as we followed Mrs. Marie and filed into the house.

"So, are y'all riding together?" My father questioned as soon as we all were inside.

"Daddy." I spoke in a warning tone.

"I mean, we can since I'm here. Lovely and Wise wanted to drop me off and pick me up." Gorgeous shrugged while Orion just stood there, smiling.

"Dad, let them be. Do not mess up her night." I sternly stated.

"I got my eye on you, boy. Y'all not fooling me." My father looked between the two of them.

"Daddy, he's just my friend. Stop it please." Gorgeous pleaded with our father.

"I was just your momma friend until I got her pregnant too."

"Boy, and we know that's the only reason the two of you stopped being friends is because you got her pregnant. Now leave these kids alone." My papa fussed while making himself a plate.

"Pops, this my baby. You focus on that food."

I laughed at my father and grandfather as the pair were always bickering.

"Here. Why don't you go make you a plate while I get some pictures of these babies?" Ms. Marie handed my father a plate.

He looked at my sister and Orion before heading over to the table.

"Auntie, I want a picture with the princess." Skylar jumped up and down, standing between Gorgeous and Orion.

"Girl, you better relax. I told your daddy not to let you eat all them sweets. Now stand still." Marie fussed.

"Do you want a picture with the pretty princess too?" Wise asked Peace, still holding her.

"You need to put her down. She is not a baby." Honor sat on the arm of his mother's couch, still eating .

"Don't worry about us. Tell him, Peace. We good over here." Wise tickled her, causing her to laugh a little.

"How are you, beautiful?" Craft whispered in my ear.

"I'm fine and you?" I turned and faced him.

"I'm good, would be better if you go on another date with me."

"We've gone on a date before?" I quizzed.

"Oh, that's how you getting at me?"

"No, I'm just playing with you, but I guess I can make that happen. I'll even let you pick the place this time."

"You guess? Oh, it's going to happen."

"Oh, you're so sure, huh?"

"I am, but would you like something to eat?"

I looked over at the table and then looked at my father, grandfather, and cousin to see them all watching me, each of them holding a plate of food.

"Yeah, I can definitely go for some food. I haven't eaten nothing since breakfast this morning."

He looked at his watch then back at me. "It's almost six in the evening. What you trying to do, pass out?" He grabbed my hand, pulling me over to the table. He grabbed a plate and put a little of everything on it. Grabbing my hand again, he pulled me through the kitchen and to a table, placing the plate on the table.

"Here, have a seat. What would you like to drink? We have water, Kool-Aid, my auntie famous Arnold Palmer, Pepsi, ginger ale."

"I will like to try your aunt's Arnold Palmer."

"Coming right up." He went over, grabbing a plastic cup off the counter. Opening the freezer, he scooped some ice in the cup then opened the fridge and filled my cup up.

"Alright, here you go, one ice cold Arnold Palmer." He placed my cup down then sat in the chair beside me.

Picking up the spoon, he scooped up some rice and put the spoon up to my mouth. Opening my mouth, I allowed him to feed me. Closing my eyes, I savored the rice.

"Um, did your aunt cook this?"

"Yes, her famous chicken fried rice. She cooked everything - the deviled eggs, the wings, meatballs. But the sandwiches she got from Costco. I personally feel a party isn't a party without those Costco sandwiches cause that dip they have for them is bomb."

"Well, this rice is definitely amazing." I took the spoon out of his hand and dug in. Tasting a bit of everything on my plate, I stopped to see how the drink tasted.

"Aye, this Arnold Palmer is good. I'm going to have to take a cup of this for the road." I drank down the rest. "Would you mind getting me a refill?" I held my cup out.

"Sure." He stared at me while licking his lips. Finally, he got up while I continued working on my wings.

"Craft, come get this girl. She needs to go take a nap. I don't know why you let her eat all those sweets." His aunt called out to him.

"I'll be right back." He placed the cup on the table and made his way to the living room.

I sat there, devouring my plate. I didn't realize how hungry I was until I finished off the rice.

"You over here eating like you were starving." Wise sat her plate down before taking a seat.

"Girl, I haven't eaten since breakfast."

"What have we been telling you about that? Come on, Lovely. You better cut that out." She scolded.

"Oh, so this is a reoccurring thing? Do I need to make sure you eat every day?" Craft stood over us, holding Skylar.

"No, it only happens when I get too busy, and I was busy getting my sister ready for the dance today."

"No excuse, beautiful. I need you fed and nourished at all times."

"Well, excuse me." Wise's silly self fanned herself.

He looked at Wise and chuckled before focusing back on me. "So, do I need to check in with you every day to make sure you eat?"

"No, Mr. Carter. I will be fine."

"Well, when we are at work, most times if it isn't because of the other stylists ordering food, she wouldn't eat."

"Wise!" I gritted through clenched teeth while rolling my eyes.

"Yeah, she work the whole day and go without eating if you let her." Wise continued while looking at me and rolling her eyes.

"Oh, nah. See, we can't have that. Don't worry. I'll make

sure you eat daily from now on. Hold on. Let me lay this girl down." He shook his head.

I looked at Skylar, who had fallen asleep that fast.

"I'll be right back, but you go ahead and finish that food." He headed out of the kitchen and up some stairs.

"Oh, he gone make sure you are fed and nourished, huh?" Wise teased.

"Oh, you hush, snitch."

"Girl, please. We all get on you about that. I know many times it's not intentional because I be at the shop working just as hard as you most days. But one of these days, you are going to crash out again from not properly taking care of yourself."

"I know, Wise, and you know I've been packing my lunch for the past couple of weeks."

"And we still have to remind you to take a lunch break."

"Alright, alright."

"Keep it up and I'ma tell Jasper. You remember what happened the last time."

"Tell Jasper what?" My father questioned, making his way over to us.

"That she not properly eating." It was like she just had diarrhea of the mouth when it came to my business.

"Alright, Lovely, we have talked about this."

"I know, Daddy."

"I know daddy nothing. That business isn't more important than your wellbeing. You have to take care of yourself in order to properly take care of your clients."

"Oh, this rice is bomb." Gorgeous joined us with a plate of rice and meatballs, cutting off our father's lecture.

"And don't think I'm done with you, well the both of you." He pointed between us. "We will finish this conversation, you being sneaky with your little friend and you not eating properly."

"Leave these girls alone." Our grandfather stood beside him.

"Man, you always trying to save them."

"These my babies, my only grand girls. My Reese Cup and doll baby. How is it that all my girls gave me boys, and my one and only son gave me girls?"

"I don't know. It's crazy how life works."

"When you finish eating, we can head out." Orion came and stood next to Gorgeous as she ate.

"Yes, that's fine. Give me about ten minutes."

"No rush, beautiful."

"No rush, beautiful." Our father mocked Orion. "I think I need to really drive the two of you."

"Jasper, these girls don't do nearly half the stuff that you did at neither Gorgeous' age or Lovely's grown age. Leave them alone and let them enjoy their night. Come over here and get some cake or something." My grandfather winked over my father's shoulder before heading back into the living room where all the food was.

"I'm going to ease up on y'all but know I'm not too far." My father followed my grandfather to the living room.

"Aye, your grandfather is a cool dude."

"You just saying that because he saved you from my dad."

"No, for real, he a cool dude. The few times that I hung with him at the auto shop, he be dropping words of wisdom, and he funny and don't even be trying to be."

"Well, yes, he is. He's the best." Gorgeous agreed. "You think your mother will pack me some food to go? I didn't want to get the wings because I didn't want to make a mess, but this rice is good."

"Yes, she will. You know my mom love you."

"She does not love me."

"Watch this." He turned and faced the living room. "Momma!" He called out to her. "Gorgeous wants to know if you can pack her some food to go?"

"Of course I'll make her a few plates. That's my girl."

"See, what I tell you?"

"That don't mean she love me."

"Momma, can you put me some food up too?" He turned

and asked his mom once again.

"What's wrong with your hands? Why you can't pack you some before you leave?"

We all laughed as he turned around.

"See, what I say? She couldn't wait till you arrived. She was just telling me to call you right before you pulled up, and she really cooked all this food because you were coming over. I told her how you like those Costco croissant sandwiches, and you see they over on the table."

"Okay, I hear you, but that still doesn't mean she loves me." She dropped her plate in the trash.

"I'ma let you think whatever you want to think." The pair made their way to the living room. "Okay, we're going to head out."

"Okay, you have your wallet, and is your phone charged?" His mother questioned.

"Yes, ma'am." He kissed her cheek.

"Okay, you two have fun and, Orion, drive carefully. Gorgeous, baby, I'll pack you some food up and send it with your sister, okay?"

"Thank you so much, Ms. Marie."

"You're welcome."

"Do you have money, and is your phone charged?' My father questioned, stepping beside Gorgeous, digging in his pocket.

"Yes!" She patted her purse.

"Okay, well, here is a little extra, just in case. Let me know when you make it to the dance and when you're leaving the dance."

"Alright, Pops, I got you." Gorgeous assured our father as he kissed her forehead.

Once we saw them off, I followed Mrs. Marie in the house.

"Hey, Ms. Marie, do you need help cleaning up?"

"Yes, baby, I could use a little help."

"Okay, no problem. That food was amazing by the way."

"I'm glad you enjoyed it. I will pack you all some food,

along with your sister's, for you to take home."

"Oh, please, I will appreciate it because I loved your rice."

"I wouldn't mind giving you the recipe."

"Hey, let me get in here and help you." Wise stepped into the house.

"Alright, let me get some to go containers. That way, we can pack the food first."

"Oh, yes, because I need some of that rice and those wings. Were they lemon pepper mixed with buffalo?" Wise squealed.

"Yes, I mix hot sauce, lemon pepper seasoning, butter, honey, and I squeeze a fresh lemon all in the pot together and let it cook a little before I pour the sauce over my wings and shake them up." Ms. Marie hiked her brow before walking through the kitchen and opening a closet door. She stepped inside and then stepped out shortly with a few to go containers.

"I'm definitely going to have to make those."

"Having only boys for so long, it would be refreshing to have some girls to cook with. I mean, I have my little angels, but they only want to bake sweets. Even before my niece passed, she was never one to get in the kitchen with me," she said somberly, sitting the containers on the end of the table.

"Well, I, for one, am all for learning new recipes." Wise grabbed two containers and began filling them.

"Momma, you gone make me a plate to go?" Honor barged into the house.

"We have guests and even they are making their own food to go." Marie waved him off.

"Momma, don't act brand new. You know you always pack me food to go."

"I wouldn't have to if that girl that's running up your light bill would carry herself into the kitchen and turn the stove on."

"Momma, don't show out. Man, just make my plate and I'll make sure to take you to bingo next week." He kissed the side of her face.

"Boy, you gone take me regardless."

"He gone take you where?" The older gentleman that I

learned was Honor and Orion's father stepped inside the house, making his way over to his wife.

"To bingo." She briefly stopped and gave him a kiss.

"I know you are not making his grown ass a plate?"

"Pops, man, don't start that hating sh..." They both quickly looked his way. "Stuff."

"Ain't nobody hating on you. You stay coming over here and putting my woman to work."

"That's my momma"

"And she lay beside me every night." He stood behind her, wrapping his arms around her.

"Here you go." He waved them off and headed to the back of the house.

Wise and I laughed at them while making our plates.

My father, grandfather, cousin, and Craft came in and began making plates to go as well.

"You gone chill here for a little bit?" Craft asked, standing beside me, filling his plate with wings.

"I mean, I can. What are we about to do?"

"I would say dominos and drinks, but you weren't eating right today. So, we can play Dominoes or cards. Just hang out in the back room."

"If it's cool with your aunt and uncle, that's fine with me."

"What's fine?" Wise butted in.

"I said y'all should hang out for a bit. The fellas and I were outside talking, and they want to run a game of Dominoes." Craft informed her of the plans.

"I'm down if she's down. I rode with her."

I looked at the two of them. "That's fine. We're going to help your aunt clean up anyways. so I guess it won't hurt to hang with you."

"Honor, come put Peace in the bed please." Mrs. Marie requested.

Wise and I finished helping her pack up food and clean the living room and kitchen. By the time we made it to the back room, that had an enclosed back porch, where all the men were, the older men were smoking cigars, Abiri and Honor were each smoking a blunt, Craft had a beer in one hand and his cards in another, and they had some old school jams playing. I took a seat on one of the chairs placed against the wall right beside the doorway.

"No, I want you right over here beside me." Craft smiled at me while signaling me over.

Grabbing one of the folding chairs from the back wall, I sat it right next to Craft. We all sat outside, and after two rounds of spades and a game of Dominoes, Mrs. Marie started sharing stories of Craft and Honor in their younger years. She touched a little on her late sister, Craft's mother, and I could feel him tense up since I was now leaning on him.

"Hey, you okay?" I whispered in his ear.

He shook his head and excused himself. I waited five minutes and then went in search of him. I found him in the living room on the couch with his head rested back and his eyes closed.

"Hey, you okay?" I sat beside him and rubbed his arm.

He opened his eyes and slightly smiled at me.

"Yes, I'm good. You could have stayed back there."

"I felt you needed a friend, and I feel like being one. What's on your mind?"

He sighed and looked at me before gently rubbing the side of my face and cupping my cheek. Staring at me, he slowly leaned in and kissed my lips. Closing my eyes, I basked in the feel of his lips. Moving his hand from my cheek to the back of my neck, he deepened the kiss. Parting my lips with his tongue, he eased it in my mouth.

"I'm worried about your sister when I see it's really you I should be worried about." My father's voice caused us to pull apart, making me feel like I was a teenager and just got caught doing something I wasn't supposed to be doing.

Scooting away as much as the couch would allow, I turned and faced my father. "Hey, Daddy."

"Your grandfather and I are going to head out." He scooped

up his to go containers as my grandfather made his way from the back.

Quickly, I stood and made my way over to him. "Alright and remember to call and let me know you made it home." I kissed his cheek followed by my grandfather's.

"Will do and you do the same."

"Yes, Dad, I will."

"Alright, Reese Pieces, it's just about past my bedtime. I can't be out hanging with you young folk."

"Papa, please. You be up later than me." We both laughed.

"Love you, Reese Piece."

"Love you, Papa."

"You remember what I said, right?" He questioned Craft.

"I got you. A man's word is all he has." Craft answered, standing up.

Craft and I followed my father and grandfather out and stood on the porch until they pulled off.

"So, can you make some free time the week after next for me?" Craft leaned against the porch and pulled me between his legs.

"Yes, I can, sir."

"I'm going to need the whole day with you." He wrapped his hands around me, resting them right at the top of my butt.

"The whole day?"

"Yes, I'm trying to show you some things."

"Well, let me know the day because I have to make sure I can reschedule my clients if needed."

"What are your off days?"

"Mostly Sundays unless I have a day where clients just haven't booked already. Then, I block that day off."

"Geesh, working women. Well, how about this? Let me know a day besides Fridays and Saturdays in the next three weeks that will work for you, and I'll just work around your schedule, boss." He chuckled.

"Why not Friday and Saturday?"

"Work."

"Oh, you have a few of those speed datings scheduled?"

"Something like that." He winked at me as the door creaked, causing us both to look in its direction.

"Am I interrupting something?" Wise stood in the doorway with a huge grin on her face.

"Just asking my lady out for a date."

"Your lady, huh?" I looked at him.

"We locked in, baby. If you didn't know, now you know."

"Oh, I like how you just think you gone tell me, and that will be just that."

"I don't share my auntie chicken fried rice and Arnold Palmer with just anybody. So, this..." He pointed between us. "There's no turning back."

"Alright, everybody, I have to head out." Abiri stepped out the door, moving Wise out of his way just as I was getting ready to object Craft's claim on me.

"Alright, man." Craft stood while still holding on to me with one hand. He shook hands with my cousin.

"Let me know when you make it home." He kissed my forehead and went over and did the same to Wise.

"We're going to head out too." I tried stepping out of Craft's hold.

"Now why are you trying to run off on me?" He tightened his grip.

"I'm not running. I'm going to walk to my car." Wise and I both laughed.

"Oh, you think you're funny, huh?"

"I mean, I try a little something something."

"Yeah, alright."

"I have to get our food out of the house, but are you going to walk me to my car?"

"I have no other choice. I really don't want you to leave just yet." He called himself pouting.

"Has that face ever worked on anybody?"

"It didn't work on you?"

"Absolutely not, sir." I turned and walked to the house as

Abiri clowned him.

Grabbing mine and Gorgeous' food, I said my goodbyes to Mrs. Marie and her husband. Honor was no longer in the back with the couple that had now moved inside and were cuddled up on the couch. I gave her my number and promised to call her, so we could make some time to cook together. Stepping back outside, Abiri and Craft were standing in the grass, talking, while Wise was leaning against the porch, now holding her food.

"You have everything?" I questioned, closing the door behind me.

"Yes, and I'm ready to get home and get out of these clothes."

"Your place or mine?"

"Mine because I know you are not going to let Gorgeous bask in the excitement of her school dance. So, we can scoop her up in the morning and head to somebody's brunch." Wise yawned.

"You think you know me so bad." I rolled my eyes as we headed to my car.

"I know you weren't just about to walk past me?" Craft gently grabbed my arm and pulled me into him.

"You saw me coming, sir." I giggled.

"Aww, you two are too adorable."

"Wise, please."

Grabbing the containers from my hands, Craft carried them to the car for me. When I was securely in the car and with it warmed it, Craft leaned down into the car and kissed my cheek.

"Call or text me to let me know you made it home."

"Yes, sir, Mr. Craft."

"Oh, you back on that?"

"I was never off it, just giving you a break." I winked at him.

"I'm starting to see that you're something else. But they say those quiet, sweet ones you have to watch." He kissed my cheek once again before stepping back and closing my door.

I watched him until he made it into the house before I pulled off.

Chapter 10

Lovely

"I've been wanting my hands all over your body since I saw you that night at the club." He ran his hands up my stomach, over my breasts, and wrapped one around my neck while using the other to grip my hair and pull my head back.

I gulped as my palms got sweaty.

"You look like a delicious Hershey kiss." He licked along my jawline. "Now that I got my hands on you, I don't even think it's a question whether you're mine or not."

My breathing became sporadic with him so close. Removing his hand from my neck, he ran it down my body. While looking me in the eyes, he ran it over my pussy. Spreading my lips, he slid a finger inside of me. Running his tongue over my lips, he inserted another finger while sucking my bottom lip in his mouth.

"Umm." I heard faintly leave my mouth.

"So hot and wet. You've been waiting for me, huh, chocolate?" He spoke against my lips. "You've been waiting for me to touch you, huh?"

I couldn't even answer because just the feel of his fingers was doing something to me.

"You feel so good against my fingers, but I know you'll feel even better with my dick inside of you." He released my hair and pulled his fingers from my pussy.

I gasped.

Stepping back, he removed his shirt, revealing a toned body with a few scattered tattoos. Next, he unbuttoned and allowed the jeans he was wearing to drop to the floor. Stepping out of them, he stepped back directly in front of me, wedging himself between my legs. I felt his dick that rested on my pussy.

"You ready for me?"

I nodded my head yes while taking a deep breath.

"Nah, I need you to tell me you're ready for me." He shook his head.

"I'm, I'm ready." I shakily spat out.

Dipping down slightly, he cuffed both arms under my legs and lifted me up, causing my pussy to rub against his stomach.

"That pussy ready for me. I can feel the wetness on my stomach, but I don't think you mentally ready for this dick." He placed my back against the wall.

"Why, why?" I questioned before nibbling on my bottom lip.

"Cause once I slide this dick in you, this bare dick I might add, we locked in. I'm not giving you this dick just to be giving it to you. I'm giving it to you to give you a reason to call me Mr. Carter. Because I definitely will be calling you Mrs. Carter. So, are you ready for this, Lovely?"

Sweat was forming above my top lip. "Yes, I'm ready."

As he kissed my lips and slid his tongue in my mouth, I felt him slowly sliding me down on it. I didn't even know when he managed to pull it from his boxers, but how slowly he slid me up and down it felt so euphoric. As he sped up his pace, I broke the kiss and threw my head back.

"You feel that?" He slid me up and down his dick. "Pussy keep squeezing my dick. You not trying to come up off it, huh?"

"Shit, Craft!" I hissed.

"What, what did I do?"

"Shit, it feels good."

"Yeah, I feel them juices, but I want you to wet me up." He started bouncing me faster.

"Oh, my God."

"Nah, baby, loosen them legs up. The pussy already gripping.

You are not about to trap me in these juicy chocolate thighs."

"Craft!" I yelled out, eyes rolling to the back of my head and head feeling like it wanted to just roll off as my head fell forward, resting on him.

"That's one." He slipped his dick out of me.

"One?" My head popped up lazily.

"Oh, you thought that was it?" He chuckled, walking over to the couch. Laying me down, he stood over me and just looked down at me, dick hard and glistening. Licking his lips, he got down to his knees. Spreading my legs open, he ran his eyes from my face, over my breasts, down my stomach, and stopped at my pussy. Nervous, I tried to close my legs, but I was no match for his strength.

"No need to be shy with the pussy. We about to get real acquainted tonight and well through the morning." He dropped his head between my thighs.

He kissed my pussy lips before running his tongue between my slit. Placing his arms between my legs, he used them to keep my legs nudged open. Taking one hand, he spread my lips and swiped his tongue over my pussy. Stopping at my clit, he gently sucked on it. Sticking two fingers inside me, he slid them in and out while he proceeded to eat me like it was his calling. On the brink of cumming again, I tried to pull away, causing him to pull his fingers out of me and wrap his arms around my thighs and hold me in place. He never removed his mouth from my pussy, and I gave him exactly what he was nonverbally asking for. I released once again. This time, he didn't give me time to recover before he was quickly hovering over me and sliding his dick back inside of me.

He captured my lips as I let out a moan. I could only enjoy the feel of him. Releasing my lips, he pulled his upper body to an upright position. Pulling his dick out to just the tip, he quickly dove back in. Repeating that action a few times caused me to release once again. The feeling I felt was like the one night I got high with Wise, and I felt like I was floating. If sex with Craft was going to feel like this every time, then he never had to worry about me not being in the mood. He leaned down, sticking his tongue out, and I happily sucked it in my mouth.

"You know you could have just gone home with the man."

I jumped up out of my sleep at the sound of Wise's voice. Looking around, I realized I was in my room at her house.

"You two were getting pretty steamy, huh? You all in here sweating, moaning, twisting, and turning. Shit, you might be pregnant just off that dream." Wise laughed.

"I can't stand you." I grabbed one of the decorative pillows and threw it at her.

"Yeah, yeah. If it wasn't for your phone going off, I wouldn't have ever interrupted you and would have continued to let Craft have his way with you. Even if I can't sleep from all the noise, you in here keeping up."

I looked over at the dresser and grabbed my phone just as someone started banging on Wise's door.

"What the hell?" She headed out of the room, and I jumped up and rushed right behind her. Stopping in the hallway, she quickly grabbed her gun that she had stored there, as well as handing me the bat.

"Who is it?" She yelled.

"Abiri. Wise, open the damn door."

Looking at me wearily, she quickly snatched the door open.

"Man, I keep telling you about turning your phone off, and Lovely, why you not answering your phone?" He stormed in, looking between the two of us.

"You know how I am about my sleep." Wise argued.

"Man, fuck all that. We need to get to the hospital. Gorgeous and Orion were in an accident on the way home from homecoming."

"What? Oh, my God!" I rushed back down the hall and slid on my slippers before rushing back to the front.

Arriving at the hospital, I hopped out of the car before Abiri could put the car in park, causing one of my slippers to slide off. I didn't even stop when Abiri said to wait. Rushing inside, I rushed to the front desk.

"Hi, my little sister, Gorgeous Reynolds, was in an accident tonight."

"Lovely."

I turned around at my name being called. My grandfather and Craft were standing there.

"Where is your shoe?" My grandfather asked, causing me to look down at my feet.

"Girl, I told you to wait." Abiri walked up, handing me my slipper.

I dropped it to the floor and slid my foot in it.

"Here, put my coat on." Craft took off his coat and handed it to me.

I looked at him and down at myself, realizing I was out in my nightgown.

Grabbing it, I put it on as I looked around the waiting room. I eyed my father, Ms. Marie and her husband, who was holding a sleeping Peace, and Honor, who was holding a sleeping Skylar.

"Papa, what happened? What are they saying?" My grandfather opened his arms, and I fell into them.

"They are going to be just fine, minor cuts and bruises. They will be sore for a while, but they're alive and will heal." I cried as he rubbed my back and updated me.

I hadn't been to the hospital since the last time I passed out from exhaustion and not eating properly. I could honestly say that after my grandmother passed, I was not taking care of myself. I was taking on so many clients because that was my way to cope. I thought I had ended up in the hospital three different times in a four-month time span. After the last time, my father forced me to come stay with him for a little while. He even went as far as to hire a home nurse, who basically just cooked for me. She was an older lady, and I did grow to love the time we spent together and her words of wisdom. She reminded me so much of my grandmother, but she was just a little more reserved with her words. whereas my grandmother just told it like it was and wasn't worried about whose feelings she hurt.

"Okay, stop all that crying and go clean your face. We're

just waiting for them to finish running tests and checking them. They should be out soon to start calling us back." My grandfather hugged me tight before releasing me.

I rushed off to the bathroom and into a stall. I sat there and cried for a moment because what if I had lost her? She was practically my baby. I finally got myself together, exiting the stall. I went to the sink and washed my face.

Craft

"I was getting ready to come in." I startled her as she exited the bathroom. She jumped back, bumping into the door, holding her chest.

"Craft, you scared me!"

"My fault. That wasn't my intention. I just wanted to come check on you." I grabbed her hand, pulling her from the doorway and in front of me.

"Thank you." She looked down.

"My pleasure." I cupped her chin and lifted her head. In our current situation, thinking about kissing her should have been the furthest thing from my mind, but she looked so beautiful, even with her eyes slightly swollen from crying.

"Families of Orion Carter and Gorgeous Reynolds."

We both looked over at a doctor that stood in front of the door that led to the back for patients. Grabbing her hand, we made our way over to him with our family.

"I'm glad to see they have support here. So, the two young ones will be fine. Gorgeous may be a little more sore than Orion as the other car impacted her side of the vehicle. The airbags did deploy, which caused minor scratches on the face. Good thing they had their seatbelts on. But their cat scans came back clear. Gorgeous was pretty shaken up, causing her blood pressure to be elevated, which is understandable. But they will both be fine in no time. Now Orion did tell me he plays football. I advise that he sits the next two weeks out and follow up with his primary doctor or even come back to the hospital and allow us to rerun the test. But we will like them to stay the night, just to monitor them and their vitals. They will be released tomorrow sometime. Now, we were able to find a room big enough to fit the two of them. We will allow four of you back at a time, and we can give you about two hours as it is already after eleven." He checked his watch. "Does anyone have any questions?"

"No, not at the moment." Aunt Marie looked around at all of us before answering.

"Okay, my name is Doctor Bass, and I am on call tonight. If you have any questions before you leave, please ask a nurse to page me. Now, I can escort the first four back."

"Daddy and Papa, y'all can go first." Lovely suggested.

I watched my aunt and uncle head to the back with Gorgeous' father and Mr. Nelson.

I grabbed Lovely's hand and led her back to the chairs to have a seat.

"Peace is just so comfortable with Wise." Lovely pointed out, looking over at Wise, who held a now awake Peace.

"That's a good thing because she is not comfortable with a lot of people. It normally takes a while for her to even open up to new people."

"Well, Wise kind of has this pull on people. They just love to be around her."

"Yeah, she alright." We both laughed.

We sat in the waiting room. Lovely had fallen asleep with her head resting on my shoulder. I had to ask a nurse for a sheet to cover her legs. She came out in this small night shirt because it was barely long enough to be called a gown. Wise was in a chair with Peace tucked under her, the both of them sleeping. At times, I resented my sister for leaving her here like this. My sister followed in my mother's footsteps, equating a man putting his hands on you to mean he loved you. My sister allowed her boyfriend to break her down so much and isolate her from her family. I remembered the day I was called to the hospital to be hit with the painful news of my sister being gone and leaving behind an underdeveloped baby. My sister never told me she was pregnant. She wouldn't even let any of us see her for the eleven months leading up to her death. But to discover that your sister was pregnant and that not only did she die at the hands of the man she loved but that she left a child motherless, I didn't understand how growing up watching our mother go through all that she went through would make her think it was okay to end up with a man just like our father. I was so angry and disappointed with her but not enough that I wouldn't have come to save her if she called. When she passed, I was so angry and just wanted revenge. My cousin and uncle didn't want me to have any parts, but if I didn't do it for my sister, I definitely had to do it for my niece, who was born at twenty-six weeks. She struggled the first two months of her life. Because of that coward, my niece was a little behind for kids her age and could not hear out of her left ear, but me and my family would not let her feel like she wasn't as smart as other kids. She was nonverbal until she was seven, and for the past two years, she started saying more and more. But I was sure people could tell that she was developmentally impaired, struggled to keep up at times, and was very quiet.

After almost an hour, I saw my aunt walk from the back with the fellas following behind her.

"Hey, wake up, beautiful." I kissed the top of Lovely's head and squeezed her arm slightly.

"Hey." Her eyes fluttered open, and she looked up at me. She smiled before sitting upright.

"We are going to take the girls home with us." My aunt came over and sat by me.

"Are you sure? If you don't mind waiting, I can take them home when I come from the back."

"No, we're gone take them. You know it's no problem. If you and Honor can carry them to the car, we can head home."

I looked at Lovely then my aunt.

"Go ahead. I can wait until you get back. That way, Wise and Abiri can go in since it's five of us. Maybe if those two go back now, they won't give us a hard time about the three of us going back together." Lovely smiled at me.

"Alright, come on, old lady." I smiled at my aunt before quickly standing from my seat and stretching before reaching out and assisting her to stand.

"Alright, you and Honor gone get enough."

"Aye, wake up." Abiri shook Wise as I made my way over. "Craft about to grab his niece." Her eyes popped open, and she looked from Peace to Abiri. She looked back at Peace for a bit before standing and handing her to me. "She is just so adorable." She stretched and yawned.

"I can tell the two of you enjoy each other's company."

"She's a sweetheart." She smiled and rubbed her hand down the back of Peace's head. "She can really chill with me anytime."

"I'll hold you to that."

"I mean whatever I say."

"Wise, you and Abiri can head to the back. I'm going to wait here for Craft to come back from taking the kids to the car." Lovely walked up and stood beside me.

"You sure?"

"Yes, because they said only four at a time and I'm hoping it will be easier for you two to go first."

"Yeah, she really don't need both of you stressing over her at once."

"Abiri, hush." Wise smacked her lips. "Well, hopefully they don't give us a hard time about all of us being back there."

"They better not trip, or I'ma trip." Honor walked past us, following my aunt.

"Honor, you bet not start nothing." My aunt stopped in her tracks. "They're doing us a favor by even allowing us back at this time of night."

"Boy, why are you always getting your mother started?" My uncle stepped back and smacked him upside the head.

"Let me get her to the car and we'll be right back."

"Alright."

"Well, come on, Abiri, so we can get back there and see our little baby."

"Don't go back there being loud." Abiri followed behind her to the desk to get visitors' passes.

I headed out with my family to the car.

"Honor, I swear if you cut up in this hospital when I leave, I'm going to beat you like you're twelve instead of thirty."

"Momma, I was playing. You always get your blood pressure up."

"Nothing is wrong with my blood pressure. I am perfectly healthy."

"Yeah, I hear you, old lady."

"I got your old."

The two of them went back and forth as we made our way to the car.

"If you're perfectly healthy, why do both of y'all have handicap stickers?" Honor questioned as we approached their car parked in the very first handicap stall.

"You need to mind your business." My uncle snapped.

"Yeah, keep fucking with me, I'ma report ya asses."

"I'm a veteran, so we'll be good. Just put my little sweethearts in the car before I fuck both of you up." My uncle unlocked the car and opened my aunt's door for her.

"Wait, how I get into this?" I opened the back door and slid Peace in the seat behind the driver's seat.

"Cause you just did."

"You always doing that. You don't know who to be mad at. That's that old nigga shit." I laughed, closing the door after buckling Peace in.

"Y'all won't be satisfied until I knock the both of you out."

"You're not Melvin, and I'm not Jody. Your old ass just hurt your back the other day. So, I'm not worried." Honor laughed, closing the door after putting Skylar in.

Alright, keep talking crazy to my husband." My aunt swung her purse, trying to hit him with it.

"Momma, you always trying to save his old ass."

"Keep on, Honor. You gone be hungry tomorrow and see what happens." My uncle threatened, sliding in the car, closing the door and starting the car.

"Yeah, my momma gone feed me."

"She won't if I tell her not to. Come on, Marie, so I can get my little sweethearts home and out this cold." My aunt climbed in the truck and closed the door.

We stood back and watched them back out.

The car stopped and the window rolled down. "We have to go by the tow yard Monday to look at the car." My uncle leaned over my aunt and spoke out the passenger window. "So have ya asses over by 8 a.m." He rolled the window up and pulled off.

"He always think he running something."

"But you gone be there before eight I bet."

"Shut up." He attempted to swing at me, and I jumped back to avoid getting hit.

"You have to be quicker than that. You know sticking and moving is what I do."

We made our way back into the hospital. Lovely was sitting in a chair. She was now wrapped in a blanket in addition to my jacket and the sheet I got her.

"If you wouldn't have been trying to show off all this goodness, you wouldn't be cold." I kneeled in front of her.

"Now you know I was not intentionally trying to show off anything. I was in a good sleep that Wise just so happened to have awakened me from before Abiri showed up." She rolled her eyes.

"There's your story, and then there is what I like to think." I stood and stuck my hand out to assist her.

"Come on, you two love birds." Honor stood at the front desk, waving three visitor passes.

Walking over, we grabbed one and followed him to my cousin and her sister's room. Walking down the hall, following behind Honor until we made it to their door, he just walked in.

"I know your mother taught you that it's common courtesy to knock before entering." Wise stood from Gorgeous' bed, smacking her lips.

"Man." He waved her off, going to the other side of the

room with his brother.

"Aww, Gorgeous, you had me so worried!" Lovely rushed to her sister's side.

"I'm okay, Lovely."

"Don't say it like I'm bothering you."

"You know you can get worked up." Gorgeous rolled her eyes, causing Lovely to smack her lips.

"Well, forgive me for being worried about my sister's wellbeing."

"I know you were worried. You always worry. But we're here and with minor injuries." Gorgeous' voice softened.

Lovely just looked at her sister before gently rubbing her cheek.

"Did you come here for me or with your girl for her sister?" Orion and Honor laughed. "You're standing over there all googled eyed."

"You lucky you laid up in this hospital bed, or I would snatch you out by your feet." I walked over to his bed with my hand stuck out, and we dapped up. "But how are you feeling?"

"I'm straight." He looked over at Gorgeous, and I followed his eyes to see the sisters hugging.

"So, what happened?" I looked back at him.

"Some hating birds and a dude that can't take an ass whooping." He rested back against the pillows and looked up at the ceiling.

"Wait, what? I thought y'all was in a car accident?" Honor shouted, causing everyone in the room to focus their attention on him.

Orion popped his head up, looking at his brother, then his eyes shifted to Gorgeous once again. I looked to see that she was looking at him as well.

"What's going on?" I looked between the two of them.

Gorgeous looked down, fidgeting with her hands.

"Gorgeous, what happened tonight?" Lovely lifted her chin so that she was looking at her.

"Man, look. Everything was going good at the dance. We

were having a good time. Then, this girl, Briana, and her minions came over, starting stuff with Gorgeous. I told Gorgeous and her friend, Joy, to ignore them and that she was hating cause she looked good as fuck tonight. Plus, she was with the dude that she was mad she couldn't be with. So, we moved and were dancing. Next thing I know, Briana walked over, bumping into Gorgeous, and spilled a drink on her in the process. While Gorgeous ran off to the bathroom, I told Briana how much of a bird she was before rushing to go check on Gorgeous."

"Was it the girls from the game?" Wise questioned.

"Yes." Gorgeous mumbled.

"I told them little bitches to move around. That's alright. I will be at that school Monday." Wise ranted.

"Wise, hush and let him finish the story. Damn." Abiri voiced from behind her, sitting in the chair by the window.

She snapped her head in his direction with her lip curled up, and he just waved her off.

"Go ahead and finish telling us what happened." Abiri instructed once he and Wise finished having a stare down.

"Well, when I got to the bathroom, the door was closed, and when I tried to open it, something was blocking it."

"What?" All the men questioned at once, and Abiri hopped from his seat.

"What happened, Gorgeous?" Abiri walked over and stood over her.

"Nothing." She mumbled.

"Gorgeous, did somebody do something to you?" He questioned her.

"Well, this boy named David thought he was going to. But between me doing what you taught me and Orion busting in and beating him up, there was just so much going on after that." She grabbed her head and started rubbing it.

"Who is this nigga, David?" Abiri looked over at Orion.

"He's a clown, but I handled him."

"Okay, so how did ya end up getting in an accident?" Abiri questioned.

"While I was beating David ass, everybody started spilling over into the hallway and bathroom. Well, Briana brung everyone over there. While I was working on him, his boys attempted to jump in, which caused my teammates to jump in too. While the staff was trying to break everything up, I grabbed Gorgeous and pulled her out the bathroom, through the building, and to the car. At this point, everyone was trying to get out of there. While we were at the light, waiting for it to turn green, my car was hit from behind, causing me to be pushed into the intersection. A car that was turning coming towards us hit Gorgeous' side of the car."

"What the fuck? Oh, hell no. See, it's one thing not to like you but to be doing all this bullshit. Yup, we are going up to that school first thing Monday morning." Wise was pacing back and forth.

"I'm so sorry, Gorgeous, you had to go through this tonight." Lovely hugged her.

"It's okay. Good thing Orion had my back."

"That's what best friends are for. I will always have your back."

'Oh, my God, Joy!" She shrieked. "I don't even know where my phone is."

"Okay, relax. Here go my phone. Call her and check on her." Lovely handed her her cellphone.

"Whoever this little nigga, David, is got my little brother fucked up." Honor seethed.

"It's cool, bro."

"Hell naw, it's not cool. He fucked with my little cousin. I'm with Wise when she is right, and somebody needs to be held responsible." Abiri shook his head.

"Them little girls, that boy, the school because how they let things get out of control like that. You two could have been seriously hurt tonight, and God forbid if anything would have happened to Gorgeous in that bathroom." Wise leaned over and kissed her forehead .

"Not on my watch." Orion mumbled.

"So, I'm guessing you didn't tell Mom and Pops all that happened?" Honor questioned, taking a seat in the chair.

"No, because you know she would have acted up in here, and she definitely wouldn't have left."

"Well, you have to tell her. We can wait until Monday. We'll let you get home and rest tomorrow, but you need to tell them."

"You too, Gorgeous. You have to tell Dad. You know you're everyone's baby."

"Okay, but I want to rest tomorrow as well too. Then I can tell them first thing Monday morning before y'all go to the school."

"Oh, Lord, y'all dad gone blow a fuse."

"Yes, he is." Gorgeous groaned.

"These kids be getting out of hand." Abiri shook his head, retaking his seat.

Knock. Knock.

A nurse knocked before peeking her head in.

"You can come in." I welcomed her.

"Um, sorry, but I have to inform you that visiting hours were over at 9 p.m. As a courtesy, we allowed you all to stay with your family, but it's almost 2 a.m. We can give you until two, but we have to ask you to come back during visiting hours to see the patients."

"Okay, no problem. We will be out by two. Thank you."

"No problem. I will let you finish your visit, and I will be back to check on you two." She looked at Gorgeous and Orion before exiting the room quickly.

"Oh, I don't want to leave you here by yourself. Well, you're not by yourself, but you know what I mean." Lovely spoke while fixing Gorgeous' blankets.

"I'll be fine. I'm about to go to sleep."

"You sure?"

"Yes, Lovely. Go home, put on something a little more warm, and get comfortable in your own bed." She looked Lovely up and down, causing her to pull my jacket tightly around her.

"Yeah, give the girl a little breathing room. We'll be back to get her in the morning." Abiri went over and kissed Gorgeous on the forehead.

We stayed and talked with them a little longer. Abiri and I went to the vending machine to get them a few snacks to hold through until breakfast.

"I tried to call you. The nurse said we can run and get them something to eat, and they'll allow one of us to run it back." Honor spoke as soon as we walked back to the room while sliding his phone back in his pocket.

"You would wait for us to spend twenty on the vending machine, huh?" Abiri walked over to Gorgeous and placed the snacks he got on the dresser next to her bed.

"I tried to call his big head ass, but it went straight to voicemail." Honor hunched his shoulders.

I set the items I grabbed for Orion on his bed. Grabbing my phone from my pocket, I checked it. Pressing the buttons, I saw it was dead.

"It's dead." I slipped it back in my pocket.

"See, you're bad. I did try to call you. But what y'all want to eat?"

"If Jack in the Box around here, I'm good with that. My phone is dead too, so you can't even call me to get our order." Orion grabbed the chips I got him, opening them up and turning the bag up to his mouth and pouring some in.

"Yes, Jack in the Box is okay with me too."

"Okay, what y'all want? Hold on. I need a pen and paper because I won't even fake like I'm going to remember y'all order."

"Just go to your text messages and start a new message and make that their order." Wise suggested.

He grabbed his phone from his pocket and pressed a few buttons.

"Okay, what y'all want?"

"Bacon cheddar potato wedges, two tacos." They both spoke.

"Orion, really?"

"What? It be good whenever you get it, so I want that too,

best friend."

"You are so worrisome. Can I get a Dr. Pepper with that as well and please get some ranch?"

"Ranch?" Honor twisted up his face.

"It's good on the tacos." All the girls said in unison before they all burst out laughing.

"Aye, bro, it is fire. You have to try it." Orion nodded his head.

"Ol sucka in love ass nigga already." Honor shook his head, typing on his phone. "What do you want to drink?"

"Get me a Sprite."

"Alright, anything else?"

"Yeah, get me a Oreo shake too, no whip cream. Make sure you put that down cause I think you be trying to be funny whenever you bring me a shake."

"What? It ain't my fault if they don't leave it off when I tell them to." Honor hunched his shoulders.

"Well, you're supposed to tell them they made it wrong."

"You know I don't fuck with food workers cause if they fuck with my food, somebody gone die."

"So, you just take the fucked-up food that they give you?" Wise questioned with her brows scrunched.

"I leave the arguing with food workers up to everyone else. Is that all y'all want?"

"You need to go ahead and add your own shake because you know you gone be trying to get me out of this bed to give you some of mine." Orion looked at Gorgeous.

"Ya some real comfortable best friends, but that's it. I'm on a budget, so this is all I'm getting. Two of everything that I got down and some ranch." He slid his phone back in his pocket.

"You need to go find your missing best friend, so you wouldn't be hating on your little brother." I looked at him before reaching my fist out and dapping up Orion.

"Here you go." He huffed.

"Just saying you sounded a little jealous."

'Man, watch out with that. But I'll be back with the food .

Then we'll be back in the morning to bring you home. Y'all own separate homes." He joked, heading to the door.

"Boy, leave these kids alone." Wise nudged the back of his head as we all followed behind him.

Lovely

"Wait, what happened?"

Here it was, eight on Monday morning. I had to call all my clients to reschedule them because I knew I wasn't going to be in a proper head space to assist them today. Our father and grandfather were in my living room, and Gorgeous had just replayed the events of what happened leading up to the car accident.

"Who is this girl that's been fucking with you? And whoever the little boy is gone have to see me." Our grandfather paced back and forth angrily.

"Papa, sit down and try to relax." I tried to get him to sit down because, honestly, my grandfather being mad had always been comical.

"Relax? What if that boy wasn't there to help her? You can sit there and relax. Matter fact, let's go ahead and head to this school because something needs to be done."

"I'm with my pops. What if something other than the accident happened to my baby girl? What if the accident was worse than it was?" My father stood from the couch.

"We are going to the school, but I don't need the three of you going in there hostile. We're going to go in there like civilized adults and talk to the principal." I looked between my father, grandfather, and Wise.

"Then if they are not giving the answer that we are looking for, then I can knock some shit over? Okay, got it." Wise stood there, smiling like she had it all figured out.

"Lord, please be with us." I said a quick prayer as my door opened, and Abiri stepped in my house. "Lord, I'm going to really need you today. Please be with us." I looked to my ceiling. Wise was blunt and wild with her shenanigans, while Abiri was a silent but deadly type.

"What time are we heading out, and what are you praying for?" Abiri questioned.

"We were getting ready to head out now. I don't know, but the four of you are already screaming disaster in the making."

"I'm straight as long as they are not on no bullshit up there." Abiri shrugged his shoulders.

"Yeah, I hear you. Let's go." I stepped to the side to allow Gorgeous room to get up off the couch.

We all filed out of the house. My father and grandfather got in his car while the girls, myself, and surprisingly Abiri got in my car. The car ride had minimal conversation, and I didn't even bother to put the radio on. Pulling up to the school, we parked and headed for the entrance.

"Hello, how can I help you all today?" a lady asked, sitting at a table at the front entrance as we stepped inside.

"Yes, we need to see the principal."

She looked back then grabbed the walkie talkie. Looking us over, she announced that there was a party of six, one of which was a student, that was here to see the principal. After being told it was okay to send us back, like I really needed permission, she opened a book that sat on the table and asked us to sign in, along with handing us visitor passes. A security guard appeared, escorting us down the hall. There were a few students roaming the hall, and all eyes were on us. Stepping inside the main office, I was a little shocked to see Craft and his family already seated. We stepped inside and stood against the walls and by the front desk. About five minutes later, the principal stepped out of her office.

"Good morning, everyone. I can only assume you are here because of the events that transpired at the homecoming dance?"

"Yes, we are." I spoke for everyone.

"Okay, I don't have enough seats for everyone. I did call for someone to bring some folding chairs. But if you will follow me to my office." She pointed to her office before heading to it with all of us following behind.

Stepping inside, there were two chairs in front of her desk and a love seat against one of the walls.

Mrs. Marie and I each took a seat in front of her desk, while Wise and Gorgeous took a seat on the love seat, and the men remained standing.

"Again, hello everyone. I am Principal Miller. I am familiar with the two students present, not too much by name though."

"This is Gorgeous Reynolds and Orion Carter." I provided her with their names.

"Okay, and how can I help you today? I can only assume it's in regards to the fight that broke out at the dance."

"It's not just the fight that took place, but I will allow my son to replay the events that took place." Mrs. Carter informed her.

While Orion replayed all the details and ended with the car accident, her face went through different emotions. But before she could respond, there was a knock on the door.

"Come in."

The door opened, and two gentlemen rolled in chairs on a cart. Passing them around to the men, they excused themselves and left back out.

"Okay, in light of what you have made me aware of today, I want you to know that I will be taking these matters seriously. I have had Gorgeous in my office before because of an ongoing issue between her and the other student that you just mentioned was involved in Saturday's unfortunate event. They had an incident in class about three weeks ago. I do not condone this behavior, and I definitely do not condone bullying as I expressed when Gorgeous was previously in my office. If you will give me a moment, I would like to get all parties involved, as well as their parents, here. We will definitely have to move this to another room. So, if you will excuse me, I need to have the students' files pulled and contact their guardians. Do you know David's last name by any chance?" She stood from her seat, rounded the desk, and headed for her door.

"It's Davidson." Gorgeous answered.

"Thank you. I will be a moment, but in the meantime, I will see if I have any available rooms for us to meet in."

We sat in her office, making small talk amongst ourselves, for about thirty minutes.

"Okay, I have contacted all parties and their guardians. If you will follow me, we will actually be heading to the library as that is the only location big enough to accommodate everyone that will be in attendance." She stood in the doorway of her office.

We all followed her out of her office and through the main office where there was a security guard standing by the door, holding it open. I saw the one girl from the game that was doing all the talking that night sitting in one of the chairs as we followed the principal out of the main office, walking through the school with the security guard in tow. Entering the library, we grabbed seats on one side of the two tables.

"Okay, so I summoned Briana to the office to get the names of her two friends that you mentioned were involved. She, as well as the other students, will be escorted here once their guardians have arrived." She notified us while taking a seat with the security guard standing not too far behind her.

"So, I do want to give my deepest apologies for the car accident, as I was not aware of that. I was back at the venue settling students down and making sure everyone was picked up, which were mainly the lower-class men that do not drive. Had I known, I definitely would have made it my duty to be at the hospital to check on their wellbeing."

"We appreciate that." Mrs. Marie answered.

"May I ask how the two of you are doing?'

"Sore but okay." Gorgeous responded.

"Yes, I have to sit out for two weeks from football." Orion made her aware.

"Upon a checkup and being cleared." Their father, Mr. Carter, added.

"Oh, wow. Again, please accept my apologies on behalf of the school."

As Gorgeous caught her up on some of the issues she was experiencing with the other young lady and how long it had been carrying on, the door to the library opened. A tall, slim man stepped inside with the leader of the mean girl crew, and a fairly older woman, who was on the thicker side, followed behind him.

"Jasper?" The guy questioned as he looked around.

"Nathan." My father answered with less enthusiasm.

"What are you doing here, man?" He walked over to my father with an outstretched hand.

My father looked at the man's hand and then at his daughter.

"I'm assuming this is your daughter?"

"Yes, why? What's the problem?" The man questioned skeptically.

"Hello, Mr. Shaw. I am Principal Miller. I called you in today because there has been ongoing issues between your daughter and another student, and the issue has gotten out of hand. If you can have a seat, I will be happy to explain everything." She spoke as the doors opened and a few more people filed in, two of them being the young ladies from the game and the young boy that I could only assume that Orion beat up from the black eye and the scowl on his face. Four more security guards were present as well.

"Okay, now that everyone is here, the students I am familiar with by face, but to all the adults in the room, I am Principal Miller. Now, this weekend at the homecoming dance, we had an unfortunate event to transpire that could have caused two of our students to be seriously hurt. But to sum it up, before this weekend's dance, your daughter, Briana, along with her two friends, Shay and Samantha, have been bullying another student. Now, I have sat down with Briana and Gorgeous, who she has been bullying."

"Sorry, ma'am, you must have my daughter confused with someone else. She is not a bully. If anything, she told me that this girl here," Briana's mother interjected, pointing at Gorgeous, "is a fast little girl and how she was trying to fight my daughter over a boy."

"No disrespect, lady, but your daughter is the hoe in this situation."

"Excuse me, little boy." She turned her nose up.

"Don't speak to mine." Mrs. Marie warned.

"Everyone, please!" The principal grabbed everyone's attention. "Now, Mrs. Shaw, if you will allow me to finish. Briana and Gorgeous were sent to my office about three weeks ago because of an incident in class. I spoke with the teacher that expressed how much of a disturbance Briana is in class and how she goes out of her way to say things to Gorgeous. So the day in question when she was sent to my office, she was saying very vulgar things as well as throwing items. I asked your daughter about her behavior and warned her that if it continued that I will be contacting her parents. This weekend at the school dance, your daughter sought out Ms. Reynolds, spilled a drink on her, and when Ms. Reynolds went to the restroom, your grandson, Mr. Davidson, was awaiting her arrival, enclosing the two of them in the bathroom. So, it's safe to say that this was indeed planned out."

"And just what did you plan on doing to this young lady when she came in the bathroom?" Mr. Davidson questioned his grandson.

"Nothing." He mumbled.

"Nothing? So, what the hell were you doing in the girls' bathroom then?" He questioned.

"I was just in there to scare her." He hunched his shoulders and looked down.

"Scare her, huh? You don't want to know what I think your intentions were by being in that bathroom. I ain't raising no rapist." He smacked the table.

"Wait, Granddad, I wasn't going to rape nobody." He sat up in his chair quickly, looking at his grandfather. "I was just going to scare her. Briana wanted her away from Orion."

"Aye, Nathan, you know me, and you know me very well. The shit your daughter and her little friends are doing behind mine, I don't mind getting booked." My father addressed Briana's dad.

"Wait, Mr. Reynolds, it will not have to come to that." The principal stood from her seat, and the security guards stepped forward, one coming over and standing beside my father.

"No disrespect, Mrs. Miller, but this girl has been saying little slick shit to my child. Now the words we can shake that off, but when my child is put in harm's way, then that's when talking can only get you so far."

"I understand your anger, but please can we talk in a civilized manner?"

I grabbed my father's hand and gave it a squeeze. He looked at me before settling back in his seat.

"Now, Briana and her friends caused an uproar this weekend. There was a brawl that led to a student's car being rammed into oncoming traffic. And I will not take this matter lightly. I don't know who is responsible for the car accident, but Briana will be held accountable for inciting a riot."

"What? Why should my daughter be held responsible for that?" Mrs. Shaw questioned with her nose turned up.

"Well, it's clear she acts the way she does because of her parents," Wise stated, scooting her chair back. "At the homecoming game, I warned your daughter when she was running her mouth and trying to impress her little minions that if she kept running her mouth, she was gone have to get her momma. But you sitting here, in front of me, and heard everything the principal said and got the nerve to question why. You're a full-figured woman, just like myself, and your daughter walks around here talking about my beautiful, full-figured little sister. You sat here and heard that she asked a boy to lock himself in the bathroom with my little sister, and there is no telling what would have happened. Yeah, I'm going to enjoy whooping your ass."

Wise hopped over the table, landing on top of Briana's

mom, causing the chair she was sitting in to fall back, and both of them crashed to the ground. Everything happened so fast. Mr. Shaw attempted to pull Wise off his wife; both my father and Abiri were snatching him up. Meanwhile, Briana sat in her seat, unfazed. Once the security guards were able to get everything back in order, Wise was placed in a new seat away from Mrs. Shaw with a security guard now standing beside her. Mrs. Shaw was sitting there with a crooked wig, holding tissue up to her nose, and Mr. Shaw had a stretched-out shirt.

"Okay, I was really hoping that things didn't go as far as they did, but during that whole ordeal, Mr. and Mrs. Shaw, Briana sat there, smirking and typing away on her phone. It is apparent that she holds no remorse for her actions, and that is not something I will condone at this school. I would like to speak with the two of you in my office in regards to the consequences of her actions. As well as you, Mr. Davidson, for your grandson. Now, Ms. Martin and Mr. and Mrs. Jordan, I have not had any interactions with your daughters, so this is a warning as I hope I do not have to meet with you in a bad light again. Now, I will have security escort the Reynolds and Carter family out first. Then, Ms. Martin and Jordan family, if you wish to sign your children out, you can do so. If not, I can write them a pass to return to class."

Once the principal finished talking, three security guards literally escorted us to our cars.

Chapter 11

Craft

It was Wednesday, and I was at Companion, catching up on the work I was supposed to do Monday and Tuesday. But this weekend knocked me off my square a little. Monday after leaving the school, we went to the tow yard to check on my Uncle David's truck that he allowed Orion to use for the dance. When we inspected the truck, half of the passenger door was dented in, and the front tire was dented in. My uncle did an insurance claim with his insurance company to see what they would do instead of just towing it to an auto shop. After all the running around and picking the girls up from school, the family and I decided to take them to John's Incredible Pizza to give my aunt a break from cooking since it was already so late in the day. We also thought it would help with the mood Peace had been in since they left the hospital after Orion's incident. Peace's mood had been off since early Sunday morning and going to John's Incredible Pizza didn't help like I thought it would. Saturday messed up her routine when we got them out of bed in the middle of the night. Although only eight and considered a high functioning, autistic child, she had her routines; she was in bed by eight p.m. and up on her own by six a.m., dressed and expecting her breakfast to be on the table. She didn't eat cereal; she had to have eggs scrambled, a plain piece of toast, and fruit. On Saturday, she went to sleep earlier than eight p.m. at my aunt's house, which sometimes happened when there was a lot going on. But when we woke her up to go to the hospital, my aunt said once they got them home, they couldn't get her settled. When her routine was interrupted, she panicked. Mild would be her just pacing. Mid would be walking through the house, making sure all room doors in the home were cracked just to her liking. She would then go back and touch each doorknob, pacing was included. Severe, she couldn't be still and screamed, and she would pick at anything she could get her hands on. We had painted plenty of walls, and in the past year, once we were sure that stage was over, I replaced the couch set in my aunt and uncle's den and my living room set at home. But she had come a long way from the severe mood and being nonverbal in these past two years. She graduated from working one on one with an aide in the home setting and moved to a classroom setting with eight other kids. My aunt said she didn't settle down and go to sleep until four a.m. and then only slept for four hours. She was back up and pacing around the house, checking doors, and touching the knobs. I could see how tired my aunt was and the uneasiness in Peace when I arrived to pick the girls up. Sunday when we made it home, I gave her her space, but when it was time for dinner, I reminded her step by step of her routine. Of course she checked the doors and paced, but she was in bed by ten p.m. and had a bit of a late start Monday morning. We made it home Monday night by six p.m. I again reminded her of her routine. She was in bed again by ten p.m. that night and up after six a.m. on Tuesday morning. Tuesday when I picked her up from school, she seemed a little calmer, but that night, I still followed beside her, and she was in bed by nine p.m. and up this morning at six a.m. I refused to let all the work she put in with her therapist and aide be in vain.

"Aye, yo!" Honor stepped into my office.

"You look tired as shit and need a haircut." I watched him as he closed the door and sat in the chair in front of my desk. He then kicked his feet up on my desk.

"Shit, I haven't really gotten much sleep since Thursday. How is my pretty P doing? Is she getting better?" He yawned and slouched down in the chair.

"She seemed better this morning, but your mom said she'll let me know how she is acting when she picks her up from school."

"I hate when my partner is stressed, and how does Skylar like her new school? Aye, do you think that could play a part in Peace behavior? You know now that they no longer go to the same school?"

"You know I haven't thought about that."

"Cause even though they're in different grades and classes, Skylar still went to sit and eat with her at lunch. So, it's like now some of her routine is off."

"That could play a part. I'm going to talk to her teacher in the morning."

"Aye, and I swung by Sheetz since I was in the area. I checked over the list for attendees, their IDs and payment. Only thing left to do would be to start checking test results tomorrow. Also, I'm sure we will have to restock liquor after this weekend." He rested his head against the chair.

"So, have you given any thought to when you will be letting your business go?"

He lifted his head to look at me and rested it back against the chair. "That business has me living comfortably, and most weeks I only have to make exchanges two times out of the week."

"You have multiple streams of income; Abiri shop always has cars flowing through there. Y'all are doing good in life and have been flying under the radar besides the incident that took place at your condo. But I think you two should really think about letting that go. You had a good run, a good ten years. I know you don't need to keep this going."

"I've been thinking about it. In fact, I've been thinking about making a few changes in my life." He spoke, looking up at the ceiling.

"I hope one of those changes is welcoming peace in your home."

"I hear you, lover boy." He laughed.

"Go home and take a nap or something."

He lifted his head and mugged me. "I'm comfortable right here." He rested his head back against the chair.

I continued looking over paperwork and upcoming events for Companion. I checked the inventory and ordered a few more cases of wine. Each speed dating session, we required all attendees to arrive at least thirty minutes early as we served light refreshments. There were four beverage choices: wine, water, coffee, and juice. Food options were fruit, salad, and a meat, cheese, and crackers tray. We gave you thirty minutes to eat, and during the event, you had a card you held up if you would like one of the serves to get you a drink. Once finished with that, I checked over Sheetz's supplies inventory. Normally, the Monday following the weekend we were open, we had all bedding sent out to a cleaning service that we had a contract with. A cleaning company came out to clean and sanitize the whole building thoroughly the following morning of each night of operation. By that Friday following the event, my chef would send me the menu for the next weekend, and I ordered all supplies that would be needed and had it delivered the Wednesday of that week. The chef, along with the kitchen crew, went in to unload the delivery, and sometimes, they started prepping. Looking over the inventory, I went ahead and ordered more liquor and ice.

Chapter 12

Lovely

"Oh, my God, Lovely, I need to talk to you." Gorgeous burst into the shop. The urgency in her voice and the look on her face had me apologizing to my client and rushing behind my sister and Orion. who followed behind, quickly walking through the shop. Gorgeous walked down the hall and to my office.

"What's going on? Is something wrong?" I questioned as soon as I closed my office door.

"Since Crazy and I only have four periods." Gorgeous started. "Well, I have four; he decided to skip his last two. But while we were at my spot, Marmalade Cafe, he convinced them it was his birthday. So, I was recording them singing *Happy Birthday* to show his mother how embarrassing he is. We were sharing the dessert when I heard the conversation from the booth behind me. When I heard a lady say, 'Gwen, I helped you and Glen commit murder once. I'm not doing it again,' I picked up my phone to record but seen it was still recording. Listen."

"Cynthia, my father is threatening to snatch everything from under me. I cannot have that!"

"Gwen, I'm sorry. I just can't help you."

"Cynthia, I will not lose everything that is owed to me!"

"Gwen, you are a grown ass woman. Your parents don't owe you anything. You killed your mother for life insurance, just to find out she didn't leave you anything."

"I still can't believe she left money to that fat bitch. But it's a good thing I was able to intercept that check."

"That's another thing. What do you have against Lovely? She seems like a sweet girl from the few times I interacted with her. Then, she's always respectful towards you, in spite of how rude you are towards her."

"Fuck her, Cynthia!"

I could hear a smack against the table and what sounded like a glass being knocked over.

"Gwen, you need to relax, but I'm sorry. I can't help you. Now, I have to get back to work. Maybe you should try to look for work instead of always scheming."

The recording stopped shortly after.

"What in the world?" I questioned, leaning against the wall.

"Hey, have a seat." Gorgeous helped me to my chair. "Hand me a water out of the mini fridge." Gorgeous looked at Orion and pointed to the mini fridge in the corner behind my door.

"Why is she so evil?" I could feel the tears running down my face. I was hot and felt like I had to vomit. Grabbing the water from Gorgeous that Orion handed to her, I quickly downed half of it. "I have to talk to Mr. Washington." I hopped up from my chair and grabbed my purse from my desk drawer. I quickly rushed out of my office with Gorgeous and Orion hot on my trail.

"Hey, where are you rushing off to?" Kevin questioned.

"I'll be back!" I didn't even stop.

"Did you forget you have a client in your chair?" Wise stepped in my path and pointed to my station.

I looked at Ms. Wills sitting in my chair.

"Oh, I'm sorry, Ms. Wills." I rushed over to her. "There has been an emergency, and I am so sorry. You know I would never be this unprofessional."

"I know, precious. You don't look too well in the face, so I understand." She started pulling off the cape I put on her.

"Ms. Wills, if you don't mind waiting, I can finish your hair once I'm finished with my client." Wise made her way over.

"Of course. You know this retired old gal has nothing else to do besides bingo. Besides, I enjoy my time here at the shop."

"Thank you, Ms. Wills. Your visit today, and your next three, are on me. Again, I'm very sorry." I quickly hugged her. "Wise, I'll tell you what's going on later." I rushed out of the shop with Gorgeous and Orion.

Quickly making it to my car and hopping in, I didn't even wait for them to put their seatbelts on before I quickly pulled out of my spot and sped off. I could feel the perspiration forming all over. Gwen was a wicked person, but this was extreme. Then, to lay with a man that was no better than her. Glen had his hang-ups but to go along with harming the woman that had cared for you when the one that birthed you could care less about you. My mind raced as I sped down Crenshaw en route to Washington Bank. Mr. and Mrs. Washington were very welcoming when Glen introduced them to me. Mrs. Washington and I formed a great relationship. We would meet up twice a month for lunch, and every so often, Mr. Washington would join us. They were a wonderful set of individuals, and besides being the only Black owned bank in the community, they gave back often. For back to school and every holiday, they did giveaways. They had free financial literacy programs for the youth.

"Lovely, can you slow down please?" Gorgeous screamed, pulling me from my thoughts.

Looking in her direction as I stopped at a red light, I saw the complete terror in her face and the rapid rise and fall of her chest as she gripped the handle tightly above the window.

"I'm sorry." I sighed and eased my grip on the steering wheel.

"I know you're upset; I am too because her actions are disgusting. But we won't get justice if we don't make it to our destination safely." Gorgeous released the handle and quickly put her seatbelt on.

I looked at her and back at Orion, who seemed to be unfazed.

"I'm sorry, you guys." I looked between the two of them

once more as a car behind me honked. Looking back at the car, they were gesturing for me to go. Looking forward, I saw the light was green, and I eased up off the brake as the car behind me laid on their horn. I started to take a page out of Wise's book and sit there until the light turned yellow, but the mood I was in, I just decided to press the gas.

Making it to the bank, I quickly parked, grabbed my purse, and climbed out the car, making my way to the bank.

"Welcome to Washington Bank and Financial. How can I assist you today?" The greeter sang the normal greeting.

"Hello, yes, we need to see Mr. Washington please. My name is Lovely Reynolds, and it's important that I speak with him." I placed my purse on the counter and grabbed the visitor log and signed in.

"Okay, and do you have an appointment?"

No, I do not, but I'm sure if you call and give him my name, he will not have a problem seeing me."

"Okay, give me a moment please." She picked up the phone. After speaking with someone, she hung up the phone. "I'm sorry, but Mr. Washington is in a meeting and unable to see anyone at the moment. If you like, you can provide me with your number." She grabbed the visitor log, looking at it and typing on the computer. "I can send him your information via email and put it as urgent."

"May I ask who told you that he was in a meeting?"

"I'm sorry. I cannot provide that information."

"That is quite alright. We will just be having a seat over here. We can wait. This is far too important for an urgency email. Come on, you two." I looked at her for a moment longer, making my way to the sitting area.

"There go Mr. Washington!" Gorgeous tapped me.

I looked up, and he was walking, reading over a paper with the vice president of the loan department, whom I didn't much care for.

"Mr. Washington!" I called out quickly, hopping from my chair.

He stopped and looked in my direction. "Lovely, hey, darling, how have you been? I haven't seen much of you the past couple of months." He smiled at me.

"Um, Mr. Washington, is it okay if I talk to you in your office?" I looked around and realized a few people were looking at us.

"Sure, darling. Is everything okay?" He looked around.

"Not really."

"Jason, if you'll excuse me, I need to talk to my family."

"Yeah, sure." He looked between Mr. Washington and I.

"You all follow me right this way." He turned and walked off.

We followed him to a door off to the side of the tellers' booth and on to an elevator. Getting off, we walked past a few offices until we entered his office. He waited for us all to enter before he closed and locked the door.

"Lovely, is everything okay? I'm surprised to see you here today." He walked around his desk and took a seat.

"I wish I was coming under better circumstances, but Mr. Washington, nothing good is coming from this visit." I stood alongside Gorgeous and Orion.

"Did Glen do something to you?"

"He did something, but it didn't just affect me. Gorgeous, play the recording."

She pulled her phone from her pocket and placed it on his desk before pressing play. We sat there and listened to the recording again with Mr. Washington. When the recording ended, he sat there in silence.

"You know when my wife died, I didn't accept it was natural causes. Although by society standards she was considered overweight, my wife was healthy. No high cholesterol or blood sugar. She took her vitamins faithfully and barely liked to take aspirin. I wasn't just a grieving husband in denial. My wife has been gone five months, and I finally get to get some answers. These answers hurt, but I can finally let her rest peacefully." He smacked his pencil holder off his desk. "To know that Gwen is this evil to harm the woman that loved her the most in spite of all her shortcomings." The tears sprang from his eyes.

"Mr. Washington, I'm so sorry."

"You know, my wife and I were high school sweethearts. She had an evil father, a sweet mother, and a bitter, selfish sister. When we graduated high school, I worked hard to get her out of that house. When we were twenty, we found out she was with child, but a terrible accident left us without a child and my sweet, beautiful Leane unable to conceive again. We got married at twenty-one years old, and the day after our three-year wedding anniversary, we got a call from the hospital. Leane's sister left her baby at the hospital with Leane's information. I did not want to take her in, knowing that she came from such a bitter person. Their parents, well, her father, said he raised his kids and wasn't raising anyone else's. My wife, being the sweet, loving person that she is, took her in. What my wife wanted, my wife got. I tried to love that girl like a father would. We never once told her that she wasn't ours, and we never once treated her like we didn't birth her. But to know that she would harm the one that loved her the most." He dropped his hands in his hand and wept. He cried harder than he had the day that I stood by his side when we said our last goodbyes to Mrs. Washington.

I stood, frozen in place, shedding my own silent tears.

He gathered himself and cleaned his face. "Lovely, I knew my wife left you something because she loved you like you were her granddaughter that we were never blessed to have. I always wondered why you never reached out about the check, but I see it never made it to you. Jason was supposed to make sure you received it personally. If you can please make sure that I receive this recording, I have three individuals - well, four - that will receive their just due." He stood from his desk, walked around, and stood in front of me. "I know I've apologized many times for Gwen's horrible attitude, but I want to apologize for Glen's as well. I tried my best with him, and my wife loved on him with everything she could. But our all wasn't enough because he still ended up with his mother's ways. But don't you worry because you will get everything that is owed to you, and they will end up right where they belong."

Looking at him, I didn't know what to say. I was still filled with anger and sorrow.

"Mr. Washington, all I want is justice for Mrs. Washington. She was an amazing woman, and you two have been amazing pillars of the community."

"My wife wanted you to have something, and we will see to it that you get it." He hugged me.

I stood in his embrace as he began to cry again. I could only imagine how much this betrayal was affecting him to have to re-mourn your wife so soon and to find out the two people you loved and took care of were the cause.

"Mr. Washington, if you can give me your email, I will gladly send over the recording." Gorgeous spoke as we pulled apart.

"Thanks, sweetheart, and I appreciate you bringing this to my attention."

"I would not have been able to keep this to myself. Mrs. Washington was always nice to me whenever I was in her presence. I'm just glad I was in the right place at the right time."

Mr. Washington gave her his personal email and escorted us to our car.

"I am going to be taking action first thing tomorrow morning. You drive safe, and Gorgeous, keep doing well in school." He dipped his head down and looked in the car at her. "My wife was very fond of you, Lovely, and you are a remarkable individual." He looked at me. "Keep being you." He tapped the top of my car and headed back inside of the bank.

Pulling off, I headed back to my shop to drop Orion and Gorgeous back to his car. Dropping them off, I headed home. Pulling in my driveway, Glen was sitting in his car in front of my house. Parking and rushing out of my car, I tried to hurry inside.

"Lovely, I know you see me." I heard his car door close as I placed my foot on the first step.

"Glen, why are you here?" I questioned, standing in front of my porch.

"Look, things have carried on long enough. First, I want to apologize and..." He made his way over to me.

"Glen, we are over but thank you for the apology."

"Look, Lovely, I made a mistake, and we've had enough time apart. But it's time for me to come home and for us to work this out." He stood before me with this hopeful look on his face.

"Glen, I'm going to ask you to leave. I can't do this with you right now."

"Lovely, what better time than now?" He sighed.

"Glen, I dealt with you and all your insensitive ways all these years. I dealt with your mother's constant disrespect and you telling me that I needed thicker skin. Then, your mother's trifling ass following up with that my skin can't get any thicker." I took a step as I spoke each word until we were chest to chest. "When that woman walked in my shop with that baby, that was one of the best days of my life. Glen, things are over with you and I. There is nothing left for me to say to you. Goodbye, Glen." I turned and walked up my steps.

"Lovely, I hear what you're saying, and I don't agree with all of it, but I promise things will be different this time around." He spoke as a car pulled in my driveway behind my car. We both watched as Craft stepped out of the car.

"Who is he?" Glen questioned.

"Glen, we are done here. Please leave."

"No, and then you got the same man that was at your shop here. Were you cheating on me with him?"

"I think she asked you to leave." Craft made his way over to us, stepping up and placing me behind him.

"Lovely, really?" Glen questioned me while looking around Craft.

"Don't talk to her. Talk to me. She asked you to leave so beat it."

"I don't believe I'm here to see you, so if you will, please go."

"No, Glen. He stays; you leave."

"Really, what has gotten into you, Lovely?" He questioned with a shocked expression.

"I came to my senses, something I should have done a long time ago."

"I see you need a little more time to get over being angry."

"Man, get your ass on." Craft pushed him back.

"This is not over, Lovely. I will be back." Glen declared, rushing to his car.

We stood and watched Glen until he was in his car and pulling off.

"What are you doing here, and how do you know where I live?" I asked Craft as he turned around.

"Orion has been texting me, and I wanted to make sure you were okay. Your sister gave me your address. Look, I just wanted to check on you, and I'm sorry if you feel like I overstepped."

We stood there, staring at each other.

"Um, maybe I should have called instead. My apologies." He turned and headed for his car.

"Wait, you're here. Come inside." I called after him.

He turned and looked at me. "I don't want to invade more than I already have."

"Mr. Carter, come inside." I headed up my walkway and up the stairs. Opening the door, I headed inside, leaving the door unlocked. I headed straight for the kitchen because I needed a drink, and wine wouldn't do.

Grabbing two glasses as I heard the front door shut, I filled them with ice, half pineapple juice and half Hennessy. I carried them to my living room where Craft was looking at the few photos I had hung up on my wall.

"I hope you don't mind having a drink with me." I stood beside him and held it out as he looked at the photo of me at my high school graduation. I was surrounded by the people I loved the most.

"Can I tell you a secret?"

"Yes." I looked at him while sipping from my glass.

"I started hanging at your grandfather's gym after school in junior high school after he came to my school for career day. He knew one of the teachers, and she wanted him to come speak because he was a successful, Black man. He gave everyone a signup form. I rushed home to my aunt, excited. She read over the paper and questioned whether I was sure because she wasn't going to be wasting her gas driving me back and forth. Well, one day, I was at the gym at the end of my eighth grade, and the finest chick I ever saw was there. I tried to get my mack on until Mr. Nelson snatched me away. I went through high school and never saw her again. Then, I was at the barbershop, the one you co-own, about two years ago. I saw you that day. You went across the street to the mechanic shop, and you gave Abiri some food and hugged him. I was kind of crushed cause I was like, 'Damn, he got my girl.'"

"You know the night I saw you at the strip club, Wise told me I seen you before. Now, you're telling me this, and I just can't remember." I went and took a seat on the couch, and he followed.

"I definitely was skinny and not much of what the girls were looking at."

"I find that hard to believe."

"I'm serious. My aunt got me braces in ninth grade because my shit was fucked up. Puberty hit me hard, and the acne wouldn't let up on your boy. The summer going into my eleventh grade, I went from a frog to a prince." He laughed before taking down his drink. "What you put in that drink? It was kind of good." He leaned back on the couch.

"Pineapple juice, one of my favorite mixes."

"Pineapple, huh? I heard about what it do to you."

"Oh, yeah, and what is that?"

"Well, I would have to spread your thighs to explain it better."

Hot and at a loss for words, I gulped down the rest of my drink and sucked some of the ice in my mouth.

"Oh, I got you a little bothered?"

I took a moment to chew my ice. "What makes you say that?"

Reaching over, he swiped at my eyebrows. "Just the little sweat that started forming above your brow."

"No, you don't have me bothered. Would you like another drink?" I quickly stood.

"Yes but make mine straight."

I grabbed his cup and quickly made my way to the kitchen. Placing the glasses on the counter, I got a napkin, wetting it and dabbing my face and neck.

"I thought you said you weren't bothered?" He pressed up against me while placing his hands on the sink. "I simply came over here to check on you." He moved my hair and kissed the back of my neck. "But I want to check out something else besides your mental." Turning me around, he stared into my eyes. "When you were at the club that night, I wanted to snatch you up and take you home with me." He traced my lips with his tongue before planting a kiss on them. "Can I have you right now?"

"Huh?" I foolishly asked.

"Can I have you? I want to taste." He gripped my hips. "I want to stick my dick inside you." He pressed his lips against mine, forcing his tongue inside. "So, can I have you?" He spoke against my lips.

"Right here?"

Craft pulled my dress over my hips, scooping me up and placing me on the counter. He stood between my thighs.

"I want to start here." He dropped to his knees, pulling my panties to the side. He took his hand, spreading my pussy lips. With one last glance, he dove in.

This was happening. This was not a dream. His tongue was in my pussy. Grabbing his head, I rocked back and forth on his tongue. Looking up at me, he kissed my clit while he slid a finger inside me. He sucked, licked, nibbled, fingered, and tongue fucked me right out of my cum. Standing back up, he crashed his lips against mine. Opening my mouth, I welcomed his tongue.

Stepping back, he unbuttoned his shirt and pulled it off. "Show me to your bedroom. These counters won't do."

Hopping down on wobbly legs, I grabbed his hand and guided him to my bedroom. Stepping inside, I removed my dress, along with my panties and bra, before climbing in my bed.

"Do you have condoms?" He questioned, removing the rest of his clothes.

Reaching into my dresser beside my bed, I pulled out a fresh pack of condoms for her.

Walking over, he grabbed the condoms, inspecting them, before opening the pack and handing me one. He looked back into my drawer, that I didn't close all the way, and pulled out two of the vibrators.

"Oh, you into a little something?"

"A girl has needs." I scrunched my brow at him as he turned one on.

"Lay back, open your legs, and don't let them shut."

Cautiously, I laid back and opened my legs. That first jolt against my already sensitive clit caused me to jump back.

"You be in here, spreading these pussy lips open, and rubbing this vibrator along your clit like this, huh?" He removed the vibrator and smacked on my pussy.

Chapter 13

Craft

Looking down at her squirm as I ran the vibrator along her pussy, I needed to feel it. Throwing the vibrator to the side. I climbed in the bed between her thighs and rubbed my dick up and down her pussy. Pushing past her fold, I slid the tip in and quickly pulled out. I did it a few more times as her pussy got wetter.

"Put the condom on." I demanded. I leaned back and racked my eyes over her body, my eyes stopping to watch her insert the condom. She leaned back once it was inserted. Leaning over her, I kissed her lips before tracing them with my tongue. I licked down to her breast, catching her right nipple with my teeth. Nibbling on it, I slid in her slowly. Looking down at her, her eyes were closed as she bit down on her bottom lip. Sitting up, I grabbed her legs, pushing them back, causing her to pop her eyes open as I rocked in her slowly, easing all of me in with each forward rock.

"Craft." She placed her hand between us, pushing on my stomach.

"Yes, baby?" I pushed her hand away.

"Craft, you have to ease up." She attempted to push me back again.

Releasing her legs, I grabbed both hands and pinned them above her head as I leaned over her.

"Why you want me to ease up? Your pussy is very wet and

welcoming."

"It's too much." She gasped as I sped up my pace.

"Your pussy don't think so. This motherfucka squeezing me. It's like she sucking me in." I stared into her eyes.

"Craft, please. Oh, my shit!" She cried out as she climaxed.

"I thought you said it was too much? Your words are not matching your pussy's actions." I leaned down and sucked on her neck. Releasing her hands, I cuffed her ass and lifted her a little off the bed.

"Fuck you, Craft. What are you doing to me?" She screamed.

Sitting up, I looked down at her as I fucked her at a fast pace. The woman of my dreams was laying underneath me with pussy that definitely made me want to go search for her fuck ass ex to beat his ass for wasting her time. *Fuck, if she didn't have this condom on, I would be a goner,* I thought as I released inside of her. I wouldn't have been able to pull out if I wanted to. This pussy had me stuck as fuck. Lowering her back to the bed, I leaned over and sucked on her bottom lip. She wrapped her arms around my neck as I looked in her eyes before we engaged in a kiss.

"Okay, I need to pee." She pushed against my chest.

Sliding my now soft dick out of her, I rolled over to the side of her. I watched as she climbed out of the bed and walked as quickly as she could to the bathroom, and just like that, my dick was back hard.

After another round, I was showering and rushing out of Lovely's house. I was supposed to have been at Sheetz at six to do a walkthrough. I climbed in my car and quickly pulled out of her driveway. Grabbing my phone that I had left in the car, I had three missed calls from my aunt and a few missed calls from my assistant and Honor. Quickly dialing Honor, I placed the phone on speaker.

"Aye, nigga, how you gone tell me to be here at six and you not?" Honor started as soon as the phone connected.

"Yeah, I'm good, cuz."

"Nigga, I ain't ask you that shit!"

I laughed because Honor, although always dependable, could be a little ill tempered.

"I'm on my way, man, and I'm sure Melody is there. She knows what to do and where to start."

"Man, you know white people are always on time, and you know her weird ass has already started!"

"Aye, not too much on my assistant. She cool as fuck, and her work ethics are amazing."

"Yeah, cause both y'all weird asses into this crazy sex stuff. I saw her last time getting burnt up by candles."

"I am not weird." I heard Melody in the background.

"I told you about that shit. Make noise when you walking up on me and you, along with my cousin, are weird. You like to be tied up and hanging upside down and all red by the end of the night. Yeah, you know I see you."

"Don't knock it till you try it. I'm sure you'll love hot candle wax on your penis."

"Dick. Say dick, Melody. You graduated from cock to penis. Now say dick and ain't nobody putting nothing but their mouth on my dick. Shit, maybe a fruit rollup or a grapefruit. Oh, and some ice. I can't forget the ice. But I'm not about to be walking around here burning."

I hung up the phone on his dumb ass as I sped down Alondra Boulevard. I knew traffic from Carson to downtown was going to be crucial at this time. Sheetz was my sex club. Members paid a monthly fee and had unlimited access to the club during open hours. Each member got four buddy passes a month, which allowed them to bring four different visitors. Some, after one visit, signed up to become a member. Sheetz was my baby and my most lucrative business. It required a lot of paperwork and biweekly full panel STD tests. Many people chose to go without protection, and I wanted to make sure I was protected. Now, all members must provide a clean bill of health no later than Thursday. The date of the test could be as early as that previous Saturday. Your first visit after signup could take up to three weeks before you were allowed to step inside as a rapid test did not suffice. You were required to do all proper testing, and a full background check was run. We always advised members and visitors to plan accordingly.

I pulled up in front of an old warehouse I purchased three years ago and turned into my most lucrative business. I hit the button for the parking garage for employees, pulling in. I quickly parked and rushed from my car.

"So nice of you to join us." Honor stood at the door of the employee entrance off the side of the kitchen.

"Nigga, move." I pushed him out of the way. "I hope things are in order while you're standing here."

"You are late for work and have the audacity to be trying to check me."

I looked at this fool who really stood here looking shocked.

"Melody must have used that word. You always pick up new words around her." I walked past him and into the kitchen to check over tonight's menu. We served drinks and finger foods.

"Nigga, don't try to come at me like I'm dumb or something." He followed behind me.

"Or something." I shrugged as he pushed me.

"Yeah, alright. I didn't make it this far in life being no dummy."

My cousin was far from dumb, but I loved fucking with him. As much as he played and talked shit, the nigga could get a bit upset when you tried to play on his intelligence or bring up his ex.

"Chill. I was just fucking with you." I looked back at him as we stopped in front of the menu board that would be placed at the bar. "Aye, Rita." I called out to my head chef. My staff, except for security, were made up of all women. That wasn't intentional. It was just the male bartender I hired didn't last.

"Hey, boss." Rita walked up, hugging both Honor and I.

"How are you doing today?"

"I'm always well when I get to come cook at the chillest place." She shrugged.

"Chill? Ain't shit chill about this place." Honor started.

"Forget what he is talking about, but can I put an order in and please have it delivered to my office?"

"Sure, what can I get for you?"

"I want an order of the lemon pepper strips, fries, the burger sliders, and a lemonade."

"Alright, got you and anything for you, Honor?"

"Yeah, let me get the crispy chicken sliders, fries, and a ginger ale. You know to put ranch and ketchup on the side."

"Yes, I do, buddy."

"Alright, I'm going to do a walkthrough, but Chris should be at his post, so if I'm not in my office, you can leave the food with him."

"Will do." She made her way back over to the prep station she was standing at prior to me calling her.

Heading out of the kitchen, I stopped at the bar and spoke with my four bartenders before doing a walkthrough. The first year after my purchase was spent gutting out and remodeling the whole building. The first six months of me being open was a slow start, but after a visit from my first celebrity client, business had been busy. We were open two weekends out of the month from nine p.m. to three a.m. Each weekend, all three nights combined, I averaged around three hundred guests. This wasn't just a sex club. It was an experience that many paid top dollar for.

There were three floors. The first floor, of course, was the kitchen and bar area. There were a few tables, chairs, benches, and six security guards scattered throughout. There were some private rooms that you must reserve in advance. The second floor was for shows and those open to having sex with an audience. There was a stage in the middle of the room for the different acts. My assistant, Melody, was one who performed an act every Friday. All fifteen rooms on this floor had mirrored windows. Onlookers could see in, but you couldn't see out, and guards were stationed, monitoring the floor. The third floor housed my office at the very end of the hallway and ten suites. The suites were for more private clients and were rented by the hour. Each suite had a full bathroom and a phone that allowed them access to call myself, the kitchen, the bar, and security that was located on the third floor. I had three guards - one by the elevator, one that sat midway, and one located near my office and the emergency exit.

One of the wildest nights here was when a celebrity client rented out three suites for the night for her bachelorette party. There was a stripper allowed in one of the rooms, and in the other two rooms, the bride got it all out of her system. Money talked, and my mouth stayed closed. Because this business required so much paperwork and the manpower, the six days a month was all I was able to accommodate.

Honor and I, because he was a silent partner, had discussed expanding. The staffing in itself was a lot as well. There were two security guards at both the front entrance and employee entrance, four bar maids, eight servers that took orders for the rooms, and seven kitchen staff. At times, I asked myself what I got myself into, but this was a dream that turned into reality.

"Aye, what are these two sneaky freaks doing here?" I called Honor after watching the camera over the front entrance and watching Abiri and Wise signing in.

"They have a room on the top floor tonight. I see someone didn't do their homework." Honor laughed as I watched him at the entrance checking their IDs.

We required all guests to fill out waivers online before coming, and upon arrival, IDs were checked and scanned. We had to keep adequate records down to the full panel STD test that was required. We had some guests that attended both weekends that we were open and some that attended one weekend out of the month. We often had theme nights like the last Saturday of this month. Because this was the month of October, it would be Halloween themed. There was a contest for the sexiest costume, the most unique costume, and a few other things Melody named.

After checking the list of occupants for the suites, I

went and stood near the suite that Abiri and Wise would be occupying.

"Well, well, well, what do we have here?" I greeted them once they neared me. "You do know y'all not fooling nobody?"

"Sometimes things work better when you're not broadcasting your business." Wise rolled her eyes.

"Right, but listen, I need your help with something. If you don't mind me stealing her for a few?" I asked Abiri.

"You good." He stuck the key in the door, unlocking their suite.

"Step into my office, shall we?" I held my arm out, so she could grab a hold of it.

"You better hurry up. You're cutting into our date night." She grabbed my arm.

Opening the door, I allowed her to walk in. "Have a seat, make yourself comfortable." Closing my door, I went and took a seat behind my desk. "So, I want to set up a special night for Lovely, and I want to know if you think she would be opposed to coming to a place like this?"

"You want Lovely to come here?" She scrunched her face up. "You know Lovely and I are polar opposites?"

"I know, but I think you would be able to sway her before I would."

"It sounds like you just said I'm a bad influence." She rolled her eyes with her lip turned up.

"I mean, you did have her shaking her ass in the strip club." I shrugged my shoulders.

"My girl had a bad day, and you niggas love going to watch ass shake to unwind. So, hey, what's good for the goose is good for the gander." She did that head rolling and finger pointing shit.

"Man, whatever, but check it. We're having a Halloween night the last Saturday of this month, and I want her here, dressed up, and in a suite."

"You trying to freak my girl? Scratch that. Are you trying to turn her out?"

"Nah, crazy." I laughed.

"I see I'm going to have to keep an eye out for you. But I'm going to help you out this one time. Tomorrow, I'll tell her I was invited to a Halloween party, and she's my plus one. Then, during the week some time, you can ask her out. She'll, of course, ask can you guys do another date because we've already made plans. Just know you better go all out." She stood from the chair while pointing at me.

"I got this. Just get her here. Since I'm a good guy, I'll comp a room on any floor for you and Abiri. Just so you know, the second floor is all mirrored windows."

"They see us, or we see them?" She smiled mischievously.

"They see you."

"I'll have Abiri get in touch with you about that, but I'll get my girl here."

"Thanks." I stood, making my way around the desk to walk her out. After making sure she made it to her room, where Abiri stood at the door awaiting her, I locked my office and did a walkthrough. My businesses didn't run smoothly by me just sitting behind a desk.

Chapter 14

Glen

So much had been weighing on me. My mother constantly calling me. When I went to see Lovely this past Friday and her rejection. Pulling in my grandparents' driveway, I parked behind my grandfather's car. I climbed the front steps as the door opened. My grandfather stepped out with two gentlemen. They all looked at me briefly.

"Again, thank you for stopping by, and I hope you can get back to me soon." He shook each of their hands as they nodded.

"You enjoy the rest of your day, Mr. Washington." I stepped to the side as they departed.

"Hello, son." My grandfather greeted me.

"I need to have a talk with you about something important."

He looked at me before gesturing for me to enter the house. "Follow me to my office."

Following him through the house, I looked around at the few changes he had made. There was new furniture in the living room, along with a huge portrait of my grandmother over the mantle. Walking down the hallway, he held his office door open, allowing me to step inside first. I went over and took a seat while he rounded his desk and took a seat.

"How are you, son? Haven't seen much of you lately." He leaned back in his chair.

"Yeah, I've been staying with my child and his mother."

"Oh, okay, so what did you need to talk to me about?"

I looked around his office before focusing back on him. "I first want to start by saying that I appreciate everything you and my grandmother have done for me throughout my life. I know at times it didn't seem like I did, but if I could, I would go back to the very first time that I remember hurting my nana feelings in regards to being upset with her because of the lack of love and attention from Gwen. If I could, I'd go back to when I was in junior high school, and I was upset about Gwen not showing up to my award ceremony after I kept reminding her. I remember you coming into my room and telling me that you can't beg for someone to be in your life that isn't meant to be and that it may come a day that their presence will be costly."

Dropping my head as the tears formed in my eyes, I rubbed my hand down my pants because they had become so sweaty. "That day you warned me about came and it cost me two important people. One that I never deserved from the beginning." I spoke, unable to look at him. "It cost me a woman that has loved and nurtured me from the beginning." Looking up, he was now sitting up straight in his chair with his elbows resting on the table with his hands clasped together and tucked under his chin.

"What are you saying, son?"

"Gwen killed my nana, and I made sure you came home late that day." I blurted out.

The tears rolled down his face rapidly as he stared at me.

"Glen." He dropped his head in his hands.

"While Nana was taking her daily nap, Gwen injected her with this botulinum toxin while she was sleeping to make it look like she passed in her sleep."

"Why, Glen? We have been nothing but good to you and Gwen!" He smacked his hands against his desk. "We never once turned our backs on you, even with the trouble you would get into as a child. You went to the best private schools, and we gave you all that you desired. Yeah, I made you work for some of it, but you still got it. You went to college. I paid, and you dropped out. I provided a roof over your head, the car you drive, a position at my bank that you never took seriously. Your grandmother never so much as raised a hand at you. Why, Glen?"

"Gwen!" I started.

"See, you have always craved her attention, longed for her to accept you. Glen, she walked away from you at the hospital when she gave birth to you. She lived in our pool house while you lived in the main house. She never attended a birthday party or graduation. And you betray us for her, a woman that I know will put your life on the line to save hers!" The spit flew from his mouth.

"I know, I know, but Gwen said things would change." I pleaded.

"You are thirty-four years old, Glen. If things never changed with her before you turned eighteen and you were old enough to be in control of your own life, then things were never going to change." He leaned back in his chair, massaging his temple. "What was she worth?"

"What?"

"What was my wife's life worth?"

"The $500,000 that Gwen somehow found out that Nana wrote into her will for Lovely."

A sinister look formed on his face as he began to chuckle.

"She didn't somehow find out. It was brought to my attention a little after your grandmother passed that someone inside my bank had been moving around money, the same one that knew about the change in your grandmother's will. Glen, I don't even know what to say that I feel towards you. Where did Gwen get whatever it was that she used to kill my wife?"

"Her friend, Cynthia, with the cosmetic surgery clinic."

"Anything else you need to tell me?"

"No, that's it."

"So, your only role was to keep me away from the house?"

"Yes, and then figure out a way to get Lovely to sign the check."

"A check that hasn't even touched her hands. Glen, I need

you to leave now, and I hope whatever you do in life from now on that you do make better choices, and I hope this guilt eats you for a long time to come. Don't come back here, Glen. There is nothing left for you here." He turned in his seat, facing the window.

I sat there, feeling worse than I did sitting beside him at my grandmother's service.

Lovely

The shop was lively today for a Tuesday. I had just finished a client when the shop door opened. Craft held the door as Skylar and Peace stepped inside.

"Hey, little ladies!" Wise happily greeted them, hugging the both of them but Peace a little longer.

Skylar bounced over to me as my client stood from the chair.

"Thank you, Lovely. You always get me right!"

"You know I love what I do and wouldn't dare half step."

"I know, girl. That's why nobody but you can touch this head." She stuck her hand out, and we high fived. "But here you go and as always, thank you. I'll be seeing you in three weeks." She handed me payment. I counted it then reached in my pocket to get change. "No, ma'am, keep that.

"Thank you, love. Stop by the front desk and let Gorgeous know when you'll be back." I hugged her.

"I sure will see you next time. Hi, cutie." She spoke to Skylar before going to the receptionist desk.

"Hello, beautiful lady. What brings you by?"

"I have a one o' clock appointment. I called and made it myself." She smiled, showing off her dimples.

"Oh, you're my special appointment that I heard about." I grabbed her hands and spun us around.

"Yes!"

Still holding her hand, I went over to Wise's station.

"Hello, Ms. Peace, how are you today?"

"Hi." She quickly spoke, leaning into Wise.

"Skylar, go have a seat in Ms. Lovely chair. I need to talk to her about something important." Craft instructed her, and she happily skipped over to my chair and climbed in.

"What's wrong?"

"Show me to your office." He grabbed my hand.

"I'll be right back. Can you keep an eye on Skylar?" I asked Wise.

"Um hmm, y'all have ten minutes." She pursed her lips.

"Whatever." I led Craft to my office.

As soon as we were in my office, he closed and locked the door. Gripping my hips and pulling me close, he claimed my lips. Breaking away from the kiss, I smiled up at him.

"I've been thinking about feeling those lips again since Friday."

"Is that so, Mister?"

"No doubt but I may have put a bug in my aunt's ear about how you like to miss meals, and she sent you something." He released me and held the bag up.

"Craft, why would you tell her that?" I took the bag from him, turning around and sitting it on my desk.

"She was not trying to cook for me today, so I had to resort to other measures." He wrapped his arms around me and buried his face in my neck.

"Oh, no, sir. Don't start." I tried to get out of his hold.

"Start what?" He kissed behind my ear.

"I have a client."

"She can wait. I'm paying the fee." He tried to bend me over.

"No, sir, I have to do Skylar hair. I do not have time to be fooling with you."

"Let me just kiss it real quick." He quickly reached down, grabbed the bottom of my dress, and pulled it up. "Look at the way this ass is eating up this thong." He kneeled down and placed a kiss on each ass cheek. Grabbing my left leg, he placed it on my desk.

"Wait, Craft, no!" I whispered, trying to put my leg down.

"Hey, beautiful. Yes, it's me. I'm back." He spoke to my pussy before he kissed it.

"Craft, stop it." I reached back and pushed his head back.

"Watch out!" He released my leg and popped my hand, allowing me the opportunity to put my leg back down. "Why are you trying to interrupt what she and I have going on?" He stood up.

"Craft, stop talking about my pussy like it's a person."

"Shit, I have to talk to her, get her used to my voice, so she knows who to act right for."

"Seriously?"

Knock. Knock.

Someone knocked on the door as he got ready to respond.

"Excuse me." He stepped to the side, so I could answer the door. Opening it, Kevin stood on the other side.

"Sorry to interrupt but fast tail number one is in there throwing up." He smiled while pointing to the bathroom.

"Who is a fast tail?"

"Wise."

"What?" I stepped across the hall, rushing into the bathroom. "Wise, are you okay, honey?" I stood outside the stall that I could hear her in. I stood there, listening to her vomit, stepping back when I heard the toilet flush and the stall door being snatched open. I looked into her red, watery eyes before pulling her into a hug. "Are you okay?" I rubbed her back.

Pulling away, she went over to the sink and washed her hands. Then, she gathered water in her hands, scooping it in her mouth. She repeated that step a few times, rinsing her mouth out. Finally, she looked up at me through the mirror.

"I'm good. It was the seafood I ate."

"Um, okay, are you sure?"

"Positive."

"You look a little pale in the face, so if you want to go home..."

"I'm good, Momma Lovely, but I could use some mouthwash."

"Sure, give me a second." I went back to my now unoccupied office, grabbing the mouthwash from the shelf. I quickly went back to the restroom, handing it to Wise, who was still leaning on the sink. "Wise, you can go home. I'm sure someone else can do Peace hair."

"She's my last client of the day. I'm okay."

"Okay." I stood there while she rinsed her mouth.

"I'll be out in a minute. You don't have to stay with me. I'm okay, Lovely."

"Okay." I hesitantly left the bathroom.

I made my way back to my station where Skylar was spinning around in the chair, and her father was seated comfortably in the chair next to my station with Peace tucked under him.

"Alright, little Ms. Skylar, let's get you washed." I grabbed the chair, stopping it from spinning, and helped her jump down. "Dad, are you coming?" I asked him.

"No, not this time." He blew a kiss at me.

Shaking my head at him, I headed to the shampoo room with Skylar. As I was putting the conditioner in her hair, Wise and Peace joined us. After sitting her under the dryer and then washing and rinsing her, I took her back to my station to finish her hair.

"Hey, sleepy head." I shook Craft. He stretched and yawned before opening his eyes and surveying his surroundings.

"Man, I needed that little nap." He stood, stretching again.

"Yeah, you were over here snoring. Glad to know the salon brings you so much peace." I snickered.

"I'm not going to even deny it because I know I be calling them in my sleep."

"Daddy, look at my hair!" I had braided her hair in one ponytail and curled the ends.

"Oh, this nice. I like this on you, kid." He leaned down and kissed her forehead.

"Oh, Daddy, Lovely and Wise said they can take me and

Peace..."

"Peace and I." He corrected her.

"Well, Lovely and Wise can take Peace and I to get costumes because you keep forgetting." She pouted.

"Is that right?" He looked at me.

"Yes, I have to go look for a costume for next weekend since Wise is dragging me to a Halloween party."

"Oh, yeah, what day are you going to the party?"

"I believe it's Saturday."

"Yes, it's Saturday." Wise butted in.

"Damn, I was going to see if you and I could do something next Saturday. But I'm a patient man, so I'll wait."

"Didn't seem too patient earlier." I smirked at him.

"Oh, that was a different story." His lips curled into a smile as he winked at me.

"Alright, all done, pay the lady." Wise announced, spinning the chair around, allowing Peace to see her hair.

"Look at you, pretty P." He walked over and scooped her out of the chair, causing her to giggle.

I sat in my chair as Skylar went over and joined them. The sight of him with his girls was refreshing. He was so selfless when it came to them and how he paid attention to them. The relationship he had with those two little girls was something every little girl deserved to experience.

"Here you go, Lovely. Thank you." Skylar bounced in front of me, waving a hundred-dollar bill.

"Thank you, sweetheart." Taking it from her, I reached in my pocket and gave her twenty-five dollars back.

"Nah, you keep the change." Craft walked over to us, now holding Peace's hand.

"Put that in your pocket, Skylar. A girl should always have a little pocket change." I hugged her and looked up at him, giving him a wink.

"How about you squeeze me in tomorrow for a bite to eat?" he asked.

"That may be doable. I'll text you tonight."

"You make sure you do that. Come on, girls." He grabbed Skylar's hand and led them out the shop. I watched him through the window secure them in the car before he himself hopped in and pulled off.

"Y'all so cute." Wise gushed.

"Girl, hush." I smiled, rolling my eyes.

I began cleaning up my station because Skylar was my last client for the day, and I had a few things to pick up. Abiri came around to the idea of his shop being turned into a haunted house. He mumbled and grumbled the whole time of him telling me I could and giving me all these rules on what I could and couldn't do. While I couldn't even remember what he said, I was so happy.

"Lovely and Craft, sitting in a tree, k-i-s-s-i-n-g." Wise came and sat at my station with her childish antics.

"Yes, they definitely be kissing." Kevin encouraged her.

"The two of you don't start." I pointed between them.

"What? We are not the ones having important meetings in our office." Wise snidely remarked.

"That's because y'all don't have an office, but I'm sure y'all would if y'all did."

"Uh, no, she didn't." A stylist, Joyce, instigated.

"Don't even. Y'all are not about to start with me."

"You should have seen how he was watching you before he dozed off. Slouched down in that chair, burning a hole in the side of your face." Liz, another stylist, spoke.

"Girl, please. You know he was watching that backside." Kevin spoke, causing everyone to laugh and agree with him.

"But I'm glad you're done with that boy and moving on to a man." Liz sincerely spoke.

"Because he was close to Kevin and I taking him out back." Wise just couldn't be her if she didn't include violence.

"Okay, friend." Kevin walked over and smacked hands with her.

My friend was unapologetically her, and I loved her for all that she was and all that she brought into my life.

Chapter 15

Lovely

"Alright, I'm about to suck my stomach in. Come on and button me up please." I walked into Gorgeous' room, covering my breasts with one hand and holding my corset closed with the other.

"Okay, sexy mama, what do we have here?" She excitedly hopped from her bed.

"Gorgeous!" I groaned.

"What? Well, you are looking sexy, and you're not even fully dressed yet. Got your little sheer skirt on. Turn around." She grabbed my shoulder, spinning me around. "Oh, okay, the wind is going to be hitting all that butt tonight!" She popped my butt, laughing.

"Stop it." I swatted her hand away. "Come on. Wise will be here soon."

"I don't think your stomach will be the problem. It's these big boobs Momma cursed us with." She looked at my boobs.

"Gorgeous, come on!"

"Alright, alright." She grabbed the bottom of my corset and began buttoning it. "Suck your chest in or something." She struggled to button the button under my breasts.

"Really, Gorgeous?"

"What? I told you they would be the problem." She struggled but got me buttoned up.

"Thank you!" I released the breath I had been holding for

those last two buttons as she stepped back.

"You're sexy and beautiful all in one."

I walked over to her mirror and admired myself. Wise installed a black weave with red highlights that stopped right above my butt. I did a light beat on my face. I ran my hands down the corset that flared over my hips. It had my breasts standing at attention and my stomach sucked in a bit, making my waist look smaller. I turned to the side, amazed at how much more my butt seemed to be poking out. I let Wise convince me to recreate Mya's outfit in *Moulin Rouge,* but instead of shorts, I wore a sheer mini skirt. I had sheer thigh high stockings with clips connecting from the bottom of my skirt to keep them up with my heels.

Ding, Dong. Ding, Dong. The bell sounded.

"Oh, that's Wise. Can you get the door for me please?" I rushed to my room, grabbed my gloves, and slid them on, pulling them up over my elbows. I grabbed my floor length coat and slid it on. Grabbing my phone and small purse, I left my room and made my way down the stairs. I stopped at the sight of Hugh Hefner and one of his playmates.

"Well, you all look nice." Gorgeous took a seat on the couch.

"So, I can assume this is." I pointed between Wise and Abiri.

"I figured it was time to tell you this is who I've been seeing." Wise announced, rubbing her eye, something she did when she was nervous.

"Well, I'm glad you finally felt comfortable enough to tell me." I smiled at her, making my way over to her and hugging her.

"Wait, what?"

"I told you she knew." Abiri kissed her temple.

"How?" She questioned.

"The lunch and flower deliveries you would sometimes receive. Who knows exactly how you like your sandwich from Panera Bread besides Abiri and I? Then, I saw the way he kept glancing at you when we stayed back at Craft house after Gorgeous and Orion left for homecoming. Oh, and the way he jumped up at the school when you were whooping that girl momma behind. You're both my best friends. I'm supposed to pay attention."

"And you were stressing for nothing." Abiri went and took a seat on the couch.

"Why were you stressing?"

"You're my best friend. I didn't know how you would feel about us being together." A look of sadness quickly flashed over her face.

Grabbing her hands, I gave them a quick squeeze. "If you are happy, I'm happy. As long as you two are being good to each other, that's all that matters. Oh, and don't put me in the middle if y'all ever get mad at each other. Now, let's have some shots before we go." I turned toward the kitchen.

"I can't. I'm pregnant!" She blurted out, causing Gorgeous and I to scream, rushing her and hugging her.

"Oh, y'all haven't been playing. Did you know you were pregnant when you were at the school, hopping over tables?"

"No, best friend. I actually found out the next day."

"Really?"

"I know, I know, but I had to let it sink in."

"Well, no more acting up."

"Nah, she about to sit down somewhere." Abiri wrapped his arms around her, resting his hands on her stomach. "I've been wanting this crazy girl for a while. Now I have her and a baby on the way. I don't plan on letting her go." He kissed the side of her face.

"You may be a young, grumpy, old man, but..."

"A what?" He cut me off.

"You know you are very grumpy."

"Whatever." He looked at his watch. "We need to head out. It's Saturday, and you know traffic is going to be hell getting downtown."

"Call Dad if you need anything." I kissed Gorgeous on the cheek.

"I'm seventeen, Lovely. I got this."

"I love you. You'll probably be asleep when I get back." I walked to the door with her following behind me.

"Love you too. Have fun." She stood in the door, watching us walk to the car.

Abiri waited for her to close the door, and when she flicked the porch light off and on, signaling the door was locked, he pulled off.

Craft

I sat in my office, watching the video feed, anxiously awaiting Lovely's arrival. I had the suite set up for a night she would never forget. Looking down at my vibrating phone, a message from Abiri came through, letting me know they had arrived. I focused back on the monitor and watched them step inside. I watched them go through check in, and when she reached for her ID back, I watched Jeff, one of the guards I had working the front desk, pull the ID back. Turning up the volume, I listened in on them.

"So, you're not going to let me buy you a drink tonight?"

"You're working, correct?"

"Yeah, but it's nothing for me to get someone to cover for me, especially if it means I get to spend a little time with your thick ass."

"Aye, my man, give her her shit so we can move on." Abiri stepped up.

"My bad. I didn't know they were both yours." Jeff handed Lovely her ID. "Let me get your keys."

I grabbed the phone and hit one for the front entry.

"Keys? What do we need keys for?"

"Oh, that's for… Hold on." He picked up the phone. "Hello."

"You are doing too much talking. Give them their shit so they can move on."

"My bad, boss."

Honor stepped in the office as soon as I hung the phone up.

"You're in here stalking, huh?" He took a seat with his Styrofoam container of food and his drink.

"Stalking?"

"Yeah, stalking!"

"It's not stalking. It's called being prepared."

"Oh, okay, stalker."

"Man, whatever." I turned back to the monitor and looked for her on the screen. I found her by the elevator, talking to Wise. When Wise pressed the button and walked off, I said, "I'm out. Make sure you walk around and make sure things are in order."

"Nope, no can do. I'm going to sit right in here and watch the cameras. You know Abiri and Wise on the second floor. I'm not trying to see their shit." He came over and sat behind my desk.

With no time to go back and forth with him, I rushed out of my office and into suite ten. I lit the few candles placed around the room and lowered the lighting before taking a seat on the bed. I sat there, and moments later, the door opened.

"Oh, I'm sorry. I must have the wrong room." Lovely quickly tried to close the door.

"No, it's me, Lovely." I rushed over to the door, pulling it open.

"Craft?" She stepped back, looking around. "What are you doing here?"

"Come inside please." I grabbed her hand.

She looked around before complying. Stepping in, she looked around. The room was decorated with black and red roses that made a trail to the bed, and two bouquets rested on the bed. I led her over to the bed, stopping in front of it.

"I set up tonight to experience you in another setting." I pulled the string on the front of her coat, causing it to open. The first thing to greet me was her breasts. Pushing the coat off her shoulders, she allowed it to fall to the ground. Taking her hand, I spun her around. "Fuck, Lovely, you really showed out tonight." I smacked her ass that was on full display.

"Sss." She hissed.

Wrapping my arm around her and resting it on her stomach, I pulled her close. Reaching up and gripping her neck, I kissed from the back of her neck to her ear as I reached my other hand under her skirt. I rubbed on her through the thong she wore.

"I meant when I said you're mine now." I whispered in her ear. "I want to show you everything your ex didn't show you. Touch you in every way he didn't touch." I slipped my hand past her thong and rubbed her clit. "I want you to fall for me. I mean, truly fall for me because I'm going to show you every day why that past shit didn't mean shit." I pulled my hand from inside her thong, bringing it up to her mouth. I traced her lips with my finger before sliding it in her mouth.

Lovely

"Turn around." He spoke against my ear, releasing my neck.

Doing as he said, I turned around and faced him, looking in his dark eyes. He leaned in, pressing his lips against mine. Sliding my tongue in his mouth, he wrapped his arms around me, gripping my butt. We kissed until it seemed as if my lips went numb. Pulling apart, I stepped back, taking a few deep breaths.

"I want you naked." He began unbuttoning his shirt as he took a seat on the love seat to the right of the bed.

I stood there briefly before I pulled my gloves off then slowly began to unbutton my corset and dropped it to the floor. I eased my skirt over my butt, unclasping my stockings. I pushed the skirt down my thighs until it pooled around my feet. Stepping out of my heels, I hooked my thumbs in my thong and pulled it off. It was followed by my stockings.

"Come here."

Walking over to him, I stood before him.

"Turn around and grab your ankles." I did as instructed. "It's on you to keep your balance." He smacked my ass with both hands before gripping my waist.

The first swipe of his tongue had me trying to pull away, but he had me locked in place. He made love to my pussy with his mouth in that very position. I could have told him I loved him the very moment he swiped his tongue across my asshole and then slid a finger in it while he sucked on my clit. I could have told him I loved him while he had two fingers deep inside while rubbing my clit, causing me to squirt. He brought my body to heights with just his fingers and mouth that I had never experienced with Glen.

"Turn around and on your knees." Standing up, I quickly turned around and dropped down to my knees, feeling as if I was under a trance. He stood from the couch before me, unbuttoning his slacks. Reaching up, I assisted him, unzipping them and pulling them down off his waist, allowing them to fall to his ankles. I rubbed his dick from outside his boxers before grabbing the waistband and pulling them down as his beautiful, brown dick popped out. Running my hand along it, I looked up at him as he looked down at me, biting his bottom lip.

Gripping his dick, I ran my tongue against the tip of it. Making sure my mouth was nice and wet, I opened my mouth, sticking my tongue out and sucking his dick in my mouth down to the base.

"Shit!" He groaned.

Grabbing his balls with my other hand, I began to bob my head up and down. Releasing his dick and balls, I gripped his thighs. Bobbing my head up and down, I took him all the way to the back of my throat, tightening my throat around the tip of his dick, causing me to gag.

He snatched my head back. "That's what you on?" He questioned, looking down at me with his face frowned up. "Stand up!" He gripped my arm, pulling me up. "I see you play that good girl role but wasn't shit good about you choking on my dick like that!" He gripped my throat while shoving his tongue in my mouth, biting my bottom lip, before releasing me. He shocked me when he picked me up.

"Put me down, Craft! You gone drop me!" I shrieked.

"I got this, girl. I can handle you." He smacked my ass, walking us over to the bed and dropping me on it. "You're so fucking beautiful." He climbed between my legs, grabbing each foot and pushing my legs back. "Let's play a game, who can tap out first." He slid his dick inside of me.

"Shit!" I screamed out.

He fucked me from the bed to the loveseat, picked me up and bounced me on his dick, standing up against the wall. I was sure I was going to have carpet burn because we ended up on the floor. We fucked until we fell asleep, and I couldn't say who fell asleep first because, halfway through, I was cross eyed and seeing stars.

Chapter 16

Lovely

"You look tired. You didn't get any rest yesterday?" Wise asked as I walked in the salon.

I looked at her and just rolled my eyes.

"Ewww, good dick is supposed to leave you with a good attitude!"

I flicked her off and continued to my station, sitting my purse on the counter. I took a seat in the chair next to my station, the sleep chair. Resting my head back and closing my eyes, I thought about how we were awakened by the cleaners after our long night of fucking Saturday night into Sunday morning. We left from what I learned was his business, Sheetz, and went to his house and fucked Sunday away. We only parted because he had to take the girls their Halloween costumes.

"Turn that up. Lovely, look at this!" I popped my head up at the urgency in Wise's voice. Looking at her, I followed her finger pointing at the TV.

"This is Brittany Walsh reporting live with channel 15 news. Well known bank owner Douglas Washington's daughter, Gwen Washington, was picked up this morning and is being brought up on charges on murder and money laundering. She, along with business owner Cynthia Marks of Make You Beautiful Cosmetics and a junior advisor over at Washington Financials, Jason Green, are said to have conspired together in the death of Mrs. Leane Washington and were funneling money from the bank."

I watched as they showed images of Gwen and Cynthia being escorted out of her place of business in handcuffs then an image of Jason in handcuffs in front of the bank.

"What in the world is going on?" Wise came and stood beside me. "Her mother, her own mother?" She shook her head as my phone rang.

"Hello." I answered it.

"I don't know if you watched the news or not, but my wife can finally rest." Mr. Washington spoke on the other end of the phone.

"Yes, yes, I did."

"All though this won't bring her back, I am grateful. But as promised, I have something that rightfully belongs to you. If you have availability this week, I would like to have lunch with you and deliver the check personally."

"I would like that. It has been a while."

"It has. I'm going to let you go but let me know when you're available, and lunch is on me."

"Thank you, Mr. Washington."

"You take care, dear." He hung up the phone.

"What was that about?" Wise still stood beside me.

Standing from my seat and grabbing her arm, I pulled her to my office and told her the full story. She was mad I didn't tell her sooner because she said she would have hunted Gwen down.

The shop was closed today to prepare for the Halloween festivities. I had two grills out, my father on one and Mr. Smith, who owned a cigar lounge across the street from me, on the other. Besides the store fronts that would be passing out candy, we had blocked the street off and set it up as a mini carnival minus the rides. We had three bounce houses, a few carnival games, clowns, face painting, cotton candy, popcorn, snow cones, candy apples, food, drinks, and music. As school let out, the street started to fill with families.

As I stood, admiring everyone engaging themselves, a pair of arms wrapped around me.

"I've never seen a nun with a big ass before."

Laughing, I turned around in his arms. "So, you just go around looking at nuns' asses?"

"Hey, don't judge me."

Wrapping my arms around him, I tilted my head up and puckered my lips.

"All these kids out here, don't be trying to start nothing."

"I can't just give my man a simple kiss?"

"So, we go together now?"

"Real bad!" I laughed as he kissed my lips. "I put my mouth on you, so you stuck with me."

"I'm trying to get you to put your mouth on me again tonight in this little costume." He slid his hand down and tapped my butt.

"Aye, none of that. It's kids out here." Abiri walked over with my grandfather in tow.

"Yeah, and I'm sure that's what led up to you having one on the way."

"Stay out of grown folks' business." He thumped my head before walking off and making his way over to Wise and wrapping his arms around her, resting them on her stomach.

"You did good. This was a nice turn out." My grandfather looked around. "Your heart is always in the right place." He kissed my cheek. "Take care of her heart, son." He patted Craft's shoulder before walking off.

"Yeah, I'm going to take care of that and this pussy." He leaned down and whispered in my ear.

"Stop it, nasty." I smacked his chest.

"Yes, ma'am, Sister Lovely."

"You're so silly." We both laughed.

"But let me see if my aunt will take the girls home with her because I'm trying to have a prayer session with you tonight." He started looking around.

"Oh, no, sir. I'm not going to hell with you."

"As long as you're with me, it will feel like Heaven." His silly ass had the nerve to say.

"Yeah, I think I need to rethink this." I tried to pull away from his embrace.

"I've been wanting you for years, and now that I got you, there's no letting go." He gazed in my eyes before kissing my lips.

I could truly say that in this short amount of time of knowing him, what I thought I was doing before was practice for the real thing.

The End!

Made in United States
North Haven, CT
24 January 2024